A Home for Other Gods

To Becky

Best Wishes

A Home for Other Gods

Michael Forester

PARALIGHT

PRESS

First published in Great Britain in 2017
by Paralight Press

www.michaelforester.co.uk

The right of Michael Forester to be identified as author of this work has been asserted by him in accordance with the Copyright, Designs and Patents Act 1988

ISBN: 978-0-9955248-4-2

Cover Design by BookBeaver
Cover Image © Michael Forester

Printed and bound by TJ International, Padstow, Cornwall

BY THE SAME AUTHOR

Books:
Dragonsong
If It Wasn't For That Dog
The Goblin Child *and other stories*
Forest Rain

Poetry Chapbooks:
Love
Light
Peace
Forest Meditation

These books can be purchased at
Michael Forester's website: michaelforester.co.uk
To subscribe to the mailing list visit the website

I

Greg was at work when the waters came.

Stationed on the 2nd floor of one of the Permit Section's building in the City, he 1st noticed an unorthodox gathering of his Co-Workers at the window. If it were the 11.15 spliff break they would have been in the staff room. And anyway, it was 11.43 and they should all have been back at their workstations long ago. Cautiously he stood and craned his neck but was unable to see what they were looking at. Checking furtively to see that there were no 6ers or 7ers on the floor, he joined the murmuring group standing by the south side windows and looked down to see the water lapping its way up the street from the River, a kilometre to the south. He estimated that the water was still a good half kilometre away from his building, but was nevertheless approaching steadily. Co-Workers mumbled uncertainly. No management memo had been received on the subject today, there were no supervisors present to consult and the staff instruction manual appeared to contain no provision for such an eventuality. Greg found his mind reverting to last year's press articles on the barrage barriers the Department had built with such publicly declared aplomb, and the increased security they would afford the City. *Life is so much better than before*, the posters and headlines declared.

He was uneasy. Departmental i-Comms regularly reminded him that *Initiative is danger!* and *To act without instruction diminishes us*. Yet further down the street Co-Workers were beginning to leave other Department buildings and proceeding at a decidedly hurried pace away from the advancing water. Did they have Full Section memos from Management that had somehow failed to reach the Permits

Section (North East, Division 4)? Had there been a new edition of the Staff Instruction Manual that somehow, he had failed to notice? He drew back from the window and walked towards the relief room to give himself time to think. By the time he returned, all workstations on the floor were unmanned as the full staff of confused Co-Workers gathered three deep at the south side window, looking down in concern.

Greg took a deep breath to calm himself. Then, in contravention of all his training and all his years of experience, in the absence of supervisorial instruction, he took a decision. It would very probably cost him his job; conversely, it might also save his life. Taking a last glance at his Co-Workers growing increasingly animated at the window, he picked up his tablet, put it in his satchel and walked calmly towards the swing doors at the end of the large room. The moment he passed through the doors uninstructed, he was in breach of both regulation and culture. No one acted without instructions in the Department. Out of habit he glanced at the Management Edict Notice Board on the landing outside the swing doors. At the top of the MEN-B a notice proclaimed that *The Departmental Republic is a happy land* and at the bottom it reassured *Be happy, for you labour for The Departmental Republic.* As if in metaphorical declaration, Greg turned away and descended the stairs. As he approached the main entrance, he found the security barriers already deserted and a few hesitant colleagues peering out from around corners. Bereft of instruction, their reticence reminded Greg of worker bees in a queenless hive, for level 6 and 7 Supervisors were entirely absent. Even at this late stage he would instantly have obeyed an instruction from such an authority, but there were none to be found. With a monumental counter-intuitive effort, he walked through the security screens. Setting off no alarms, he half walked, half ran, straight out of the building.

Resisting the urge to fall in with the panic he saw all around him,

Greg turned away from the water to head north in the direction of home, the terrain rising as he fled. Approaching the City Transport Terminal, to his considerable surprise, Greg found the system still functioning. The Terminal staff, though looking clearly uneasy at the unusual amount of Suburbia-bound traffic for this time of the morning, had evidently received no instruction to stop the Transporters. To Greg's great relief he jumped on a tram just as the doors were closing. As it pulled out of the Station he watched hordes of panicking Co-Workers storm onto the platform, some falling onto the live rails of the track.

As the tram glided silently towards Suburbia 14, Greg's only thoughts were for the safety of his family. His wife, Grete, worked as a level 3 medic in the Co-Workers Health Facility, a kilometre from their home. At 8 years of age, their pride and joy, Joe, attended the Co-Students Primary Learning Facility next door. Both these facilities and their home were on higher ground than the City, so there was little logical reason to worry just yet. The tram passed the ancient ruined mythical-deity worship facility and the abandoned retail park that the Department had closed back in '91 (*retail is an unnecessary evil*). Somehow Greg remained profoundly uneasy. His eyes alighted on the tram's comms link. It featured the Department's current inspirational message – '*Ask not what the Department can do for you. Ask what you can do for the Department.*'

Arriving at the Suburbia 14 Terminal, Greg and the other Co-Workers poured from the carriage. He literally ran to his LivUnit and pressed his palm against the lock. The door slid back just as it always did. "Grete?" he yelled out. There was no answer, but he could hear the SkypeWAll playing loudly in the lounge. As he rushed into the room he found Grete and Joe absorbed in the Channel 1 DepCast.

His wife turned to him with shining eyes. "Isn't it wonderful?" she cried in genuine excitement.

3

Greg was overcome with relief to see his family together and unharmed. "Isn't what wonderful?" he managed to stutter out.

"You've not heard the news?" asked Grete, "the news about the referendum?"

"What news? What referendum? Tell me what's happening."

"The Oceanic Union, silly," she replied in amusement. "The Department has announced they have negotiated terms for us to join the OU and we are to have a referendum."

"What Union?" Greg responded in confusion. "Grete, I haven't a clue what you're talking about."

"Where has your head been these last few months, my sweet Co-Worker?" she giggled.

"Oh, Pop!" cried Joe. "Everyone knows the Department discovered the Oceanic Union years ago."

Greg's wife looked at him with an expression somewhere between love and despair. "The DepCasts have been reminding us because the Department knows airheads like you will have forgotten. All the Co-Students and co-students got sent home this morning to watch the DepCasts. Bless the Department. It's so exciting!"

"Look, Pop!" interjected Joe again, holding up his i-Comm. Greg looked at his son's drawing, no less confused than he had been at his wife's explanation.

"Err, lovely, Joe. What is it?"

"It's a Fishperson, of course, Pop! Everyone at EdFac's talking about the Fishpersons. And I'm Ed Group rep for the OU this week. Look – I've got a badge." Greg looked at his son's badge which did indeed bear the words 'OU Education Group Rep'.

"A Fishperson?" Greg replied, looking at the coloured drawing on his son's screen. As far as he could tell, it was a just a fish head on a human body.

"Yes," his son insisted. "It's a Co-Worker from Oceanic Union.

They're amazing! They can swim just by moving their feet. And they can breathe under water an' talk Fishspeak an'... an' everything! They're sooo clever! Co-Educator Sam says they'll be arriving soon and we have to draw pictures to welcome them. Look, Pop. I can sing the Oceanic Anthem already. It goes like this." Greg watched as his son stood solemnly to attention, opening and closing his mouth soundlessly. "Isn't it great?" Joe asked excitedly.

Greg was now uncertain. Had there really been announcements by the Department about all this? And was it connected in some way to the water rising in the City? He didn't know what to think. But then, again, there had been so much he had failed to remember recently, anyway. Perhaps, they were right. If the Department said it was so, it must be, mustn't it? The fault must lie with him. Despite his doubts, Greg smiled and said, "Yes, that's amazing, Joe! I remember now. How silly of me to forget. The Oceanic Union. How marvellous that the Department has made yet more wonderful improvements in our lives."

II

That night in bed, Greg lay awake. The blackout blinds were not a perfect fit, and moonlight was edging its way into the room. The Department's Handy Guide to Daily Living recommended an 11.00 pm retiring time for adults, immediately after the Channel 1 late DepCast, followed by half an hour of reading recommended by the Departmental Area Reading Group (or, as the manual specified, half an hour of procreative activity may be guiltlessly substituted by those in possession of permits to undertake nuclear living group expansion). Greg followed the advice for non-NLG expanders, but the Departmental expectation of eight hours continuous sleep inexplicably failed to arrive. He knew the fault must lie with him. It always did. But today, he had seemed to come so close to losing what he most valued. And these very people who mattered so much to him were adamant that the Department had been making the claimed announcements for months, so, why couldn't he remember them? He wished he was better at following Departmental admonitions and aphorisms. Though he avoided voicing it, despite his past troubles, Conformity was not as instinctive with Greg as both he and the Department would have wished. That was what had led to all the pain and sadness 15 years back. And with this latest worry, perhaps he was just getting old. He tried to avoid thinking about it, but perhaps this was the 1st indication of early onset Alzheimer's. And that would mean that… He stopped himself short. Even thinking about it was dangerous.

Greg allowed his mind to drift back over the years. He thought of the time when he finished his co-ed back in '83. Like everyone else he had aspired to join one of the Companies. But he had achieved only one PhD, grossly disappointing his parents and failing to distinguish himself from the rest of the crop of that year's work-seekers. All the Companies he had applied to had passed him over in favour of more impressive double and triple PhDs. But he'd got over the disappointment, and so eventually, had his parents. Anyway, it didn't really matter, because the Department had been dysoning up every new starter they could find in those days, even if his CV didn't buy him a managerial level appointment. In the end, it had become irrelevant. Within ten years, the Department had grown so rapidly and taxed the Companies so heavily that when they finally announced they would be Admitting the Companies for the good of all, it seemed like the obvious course of action. Company Admission Day had been declared a Departmental Holiday, when everyone could spend a few recreative hours studying a Departmental Personal Improvement Manual, or maybe taking their NLG to a picnic area to enjoy the Departmentally provided sunshine.

Greg's Departmental career had commenced in Travel Permits – Section 4 – Group 6 on the ground floor of one of the Section's building in the north of the City. Starting as a Level 1 Operative, his job had been to assess and authorise Travel Permit Applications from Co-Workers who needed to venture beyond the Suburban ring on behalf of the Department. He and the other Level 1-3 Operatives would authorise the Applications with an official Department stamp and pass them in batches to Level 4 Supervisors who would 75% sample the batch and counter stamp them before passing them to Level 5 Supervisors. Lev 5-ers held the real power on the floor. They would sample only a further 25% and counter stamp them before passing them to a Level 6 Manager who would undertake a final check before passing to Level 7 Managers for authorisation. Level 6 Managers were an uncommon sight on Greg's floor. He had never knowingly seen a Level 7 Manager.

After Greg had been working in the Permits Section for 18 months, a sequence of events had occurred that was to have a profound significance upon him. It started with an i-Comm, confirming his elevation to Level 2 Operative, effective 6 months hence. That night, when he told his parents his mother had cried. "Finally," she had said, stroking his face and hugging him close. "Finally, I have a son to be proud of!" She had scuttled off to tell Co-Worker, Mrs. Cooper who lived next door, the wonderful news. Mrs

Jones' son was still just a Level 1 Operative after 19 months working for the Department and had received no such i-Comm.

In her absence, Greg's father had wiped a tear and shaken him by the hand. "I'm proud of you, boy," he had said, his eyes confirming that he truly meant what he said. "And I have a gift for you to mark this wonderful event." With both hands, he offered a large box to Greg. "Go on son," he said with obvious pride. "Look inside."

Greg opened the box, glancing from his father's excited face to the contents and back again. "Dad, no, not this," he said in astonishment. "Not your Elapsed Departmental Leave Application collection. I can't take it, Dad. It's too valuable."

His father shuffled and stood a little straighter. "Yes. Yes, you can, boy. You can take it. You're custodian of it now. You're a full-grown man and a pending Level 2 Operative. There's nothing you can't achieve for the Department with enough Compliance and hard work. And there's something else on my mind to say to you now, Greg. It's time for you to find yourself your 1st co-spouse and apply for a Departmental LivUnit of your own. Man, woman, Binary – whatever your preference. But the Department recommends we find a 1st co-spouse at around 30 and you're already 6 months over that. People need to see you moving forward in your Compliance, Greg. You mustn't let the AstroTurf get laid under your feet now you're getting some momentum behind you." Greg nodded silently. "And besides," he continued, "your mother and I aren't getting any younger. Retirement will be upon us before we know it."

"Dad!" exclaimed Greg. "You can't possibly mean that. You and mum have years of Compliant service still to offer The Department. No one in their right minds would think of Retiring either of you yet." His father looked at him but did not answer.

That night Greg had unpacked the handbound parking permit books onto the shelves in his Partition. He stood back and looked at them. They were a fine adornment to his collection of antique books. To one side of them he placed his pre-Departmental classics – Orwell's 1984 (he owned 7 copies, all different editions), Kafka's Metamorphosis Reversed, Marquez's 100 Years of Plenitude amongst others. On the other side, he placed his collection of hand-writeable antique notebooks. These brought particular pleasure to Greg, who would carry one at all times, together with a real ballpoint pen, making notes on what he saw, what he heard, his thoughts, anything really, for no particular purpose. Unsoiled notebooks and working pens were not easy to come by and he found himself spending many Thalers on good examples when he came across them in the artefact shops at the Malls. When he had finished lining the shelves, he stood back to admire his much expanded collection. He had gone to bed happy that night. His parents were proud of him. The Department was pleased with his work. Surely, he was charmed. His was to be a life of consequence. He would devote his years to helping the Department make The Republic a better place.

The next morning, still in an animated state from all the excitement of the night before, it occurred to Greg on his journey into the City that there was no provision in the Permit Section's procedures for rejection or reconsideration of Permit Applications. Later at work, it had further occurred to him that in the 18 months he had been in the TP Section, he had never had cause to reject an Application, nor even received a rejected application back from a Supervisor. In fact, thinking about it, all he had ever been told to do was to stamp each application with the 'Level 1 approved' stamp and batch them in 50s for his Level 4 supervisor. 'Wouldn't it be better to effect some sort of check on them 1st?' wondered Greg. 'And if they're not right, possibly to reject them?' His weekly staff Supervision was due that afternoon with Personnel, so he decided to raise the matter there. Perhaps this might be his chance to begin moving forward at an accelerated pace. Perhaps, eventually, he might even see a Management position beckoning to him.

"Is there anything else?" the Supervisor had asked, drawing the interview towards an expected close.

"Well, actually, yes," Greg had answered. "I've noticed that no rejection of TP applications seems to have occurred since I've arrived here. I'm wondering

if the Section would like me to draft a system – in my own time of course."
The Personnel Manager had looked at him strangely and said nothing, simply
nodding towards the door to indicate the conclusion of the interview.

The next morning, Greg's in-box had contained an i-Comm inviting his
attendance at a meeting in the Regulatory Division on the 7th floor. In the whole
of his 18 months in the Section, Greg had never had cause to go above the 2nd
floor. The invitation specified attendance at 09.30 in room 101. He had smiled
at the coincidence. George Orwell was his favourite pre-Departmental writer.
He cried every time he read about the surprise birthday celebration the Party
had staged for Winston Smith in room 101. Ancient fiction it may well have
been, but to Greg it somehow encapsulated the spirit of the Department and
its care for every Co-Worker. Obviously, the room number on the invitation was
no more than a coincidence, but it was a happy one nevertheless. And he didn't
give any real thought to the instruction contained in the e-mail to discuss the
meeting with no one. Greg was a loner and there was no one at work he wanted
to talk to anyway. He was excited. He was sure he was being invited to discuss
his proposal. This could be his big career break.

Arriving a little breathless at the 7th floor from the stair climb, he had
pushed on the swing door, but found it locked. Looking around him, he saw
a small surveillance camera aimed down at him from its mount on the
doorframe. Greg understood the need for security – after all, he passed
through the screening system in the reception hall twice every day. He had
looked enquiringly at the camera until the electronic door lock buzzed. When
he pressed on the door again, it had swung easily open at his touch, then
closed silently behind him until the lock clicked into place once more. Inside,
he found himself in a corridor with bare grey walls and doors numbered from
100, the 1st door on his left. He had looked immediately at the 2nd door on
the left. The number on the door said 102. Then, he had looked at the door
opposite number 100. The number was 124. Greg had frowned a little. He
had looked around for someone to ask, but the corridor was deserted. He had
glanced at his i-Comm. It said 09.29, precisely. He had one minute to make
the specified meeting time, but the room was not where it should be.

Greg had moved uncertainly down the corridor. Eventually he was able to see one door ajar a little ahead of him. When he reached the door, he had seen it had no number. Instead it bore a notice: 'Level 7 Operatives only permitted'. Greg looked around again, but there was still no one to be seen. Then, he heard a sound coming from inside the room. Unmistakeably, he could hear low voices. Greg had at 1ˢᵗ hesitated, then knocked. The voices had stopped immediately; then, nothing. He knocked again, this time letting his knuckles push the door slightly wider open. Still no sound came from inside. Plucking up his courage, he had called out, "I'm so sorry to disturb you, but can you help me, please." He had waited a moment, straining to listen for any sound at all coming from inside, but there was none. "I'm looking for room 101," he had called out. Then, he had knocked again, once more allowing his knuckles to linger on the door, pushing it back just a little further. Though he had been standing centrally in front of the door, he had now pushed it sufficiently to be able to see inside if he moved a little to his left.

Cautiously, he had shifted his position slightly to where he could look into the room. He had been expecting to see at least two people, half thinking it might be a recreation room reserved for LevSevs only. His eyes had taken in the room: grey walls, grey ceiling, grey plastic tiled floor. In the centre of the room was a grey table. There were no chairs and no one in the room. On the table, he had seen a small speaker and an envelope. Greg understood immediately that the voices had emanated from the speaker, which was now silent. Checking the corridor again for someone to consult, he found it still deserted and edged slowly into the room. Only when he was fully inside and able to turn around had he seen the two small security cams mounted on the doorframe, pointing into the room. "Can you help me, please?" He had addressed his words at the camera feeling rather foolish. "I'm looking for room 101." There had been no response from the speaker on the grey table. Greg had turned from the cameras and, still glancing around, made his way uncertainly towards the table. The envelope, the one he had seen from the doorway, was addressed to him.

Greg had immediately picked it up and torn it open. Inside was a single piece of Departmental headed notepaper. On the notepaper was typed:

11

Record of Compliance Investigation of Level 1 Operative
Greg Workman

Postulations:	*REDACTED*
Findings:	*REDACTED*
Level of Concern:	*REDACTED*
Improvement Opportunity:	*Deceleration of promotion by 1 year*
	Further consideration
Appeal Procedure:	*None*

Greg did not recall leaving the room. But he did remember standing outside, looking at the paper for a long time. Then, he left the floor and returned to his workstation. No one spoke to him. That evening at home, he had broken the news to his distraught parents. His mother had supressed her sobs with her right hand held over her mouth. His father, saying not a word, walked directly to Greg's Partition, picked the Elapsed Departmental Leave Applications from the bookshelves and walked with them to his and his co-spouse's own Partition. Greg had woken the next morning to a silent house. He had gone to work and concentrated on his permit authorisations as best he could. When he returned home that evening, all his possessions were packed and on the doorstep. His palm print would not open the door of the LivUnit.

III

Following a fitful night, Greg woke early the next morning and attended for Neighbourhood Physical in front of the SkypeWAll. The WAll was showing scenes of snow-capped mountains rising up from sun-filled grasslands where happy, smiling people undertook enthusiastic star jumps and determined press-ups. Greg had long since ceased wondering why this process was referred to as 'Neighbourhood,' since there were no mountains like this anywhere near where he lived and he recognised no one in the happy exercising group as a neighbour. In fact, the whole happy group of twenty-somethings seemed to be proud possessors of Departmentally Compliant bodies that curved and rippled in all the right places at all the right times. Greg did not need to look at the mirrored part of the SkypeWAll to realise that his own body, even allowing for age, was a little less Compliant than those on the screen.

Greg's Physicals and Cleansings were electronically signed off as compliant with Departmental standards. For Nutrition, he scored, 'Good', having forgone his bread ration in favour of plain yoghurt. He then left for work, carrying his satchel which contained his tablet. Out of habit, he checked his i-Comm to ensure he would make the transport tram in time to be at his desk by 09.15. Boarding the tram, he found his thoughts oscillating between what he might find on arrival in the flooded City and the forthcoming referendum on merger with the Oceanic Union. He did not have long to wait on either count.

Alighting from the tram at the North City Terminal, he made his way forward curiously. Rounding the final turn some 100 metres from his building, he came upon not only the water, but also a hastily constructed jetty where boatmen were ferrying boatloads of commuters to various Departmental buildings. "Departing for Travel Permits Section 4 Building," called a voice just ahead of him. Greg hastened towards the voice to find himself in front of an open boat with rows of strutted seating from front to back. It looked as though it would hold around 20 and it was almost full.

"Come on, Co-Worker!" said a voice from behind him. "We've all got to get to work by 09.15. Travel Permits don't authorise themselves you know!" Greg found himself jostled into the boat which departed immediately towards his building. As the little vessel drew closer, he could see that the building was flooded to just below 1st floor level. It appeared to have suffered no other calamity. On arrival, the boat tied up at an open window and those in front of him climbed through, as if the whole process was habitual to them. No one gossiped about the change. No one commented on anything unusual. Greg followed the others into the building. The security screens had been re-sited on the 1st floor landing. He passed through, glanced at the water on the stairs lapping one step below the 1st floor and walked up to the 2nd. Reaching the landing, he glanced at the MEN-B. The notice at the top now proclaimed that *The Oceanic Union is a happy union*, and at the bottom it advised *Vote 'YES' to the Oceanic Union merger!* "Wonderful, isn't it Co-Worker!" said a cheerful voice from behind. "You'll soon be voting to become a part of the greatest union in the world. Aren't you glad to have lived long enough see this amazing day?" Greg swung round in surprise. Behind him stood a young woman with shoulder-length curly black hair, standing 155 centimetres. Greg found her attractive, but not classically beautiful. She wore a short white dress that was adorned with a large red tick on the front of it. Greg stared at the woman, not quite knowing what to say. "My name's Tick. I'm a vote!" she said with an engaging smile as she spread her arms out to display the red tick on her chest. "You can cast me in the referendum. Remember to vote 'yes' for the merger with the Oceanic Union!" And with that she leant forward and kissed Greg lightly on the cheek, pressing a sheet of paper into his hand. Greg watched her saunter off through the swing doors with an exaggerated wiggle of her bottom. He looked down at the paper. On one side was written *Cast your vote for a better world* in bold black letters across a big red tick. On the other, there was an even larger red tick with the words 'Vote Yes' written across it. Bemused and shaking his head slightly, Greg followed the woman in through the swing doors and walked towards his workstation. Oddly, she was nowhere to be seen.

Settling in at his desk he tapped the screen. It lit up in the normal way, but failed to play the Departmental Republic Anthem as usual. Instead, Greg was taken aback to find himself looking at a picture of what appeared to be a large choir under the direction of a baton-wielding choirmaster. As the choir master solemnly kept time with his baton, each member of the choir silently opened and closed their mouth in time to its swing. Greg checked the sound connection on his workstation. It was properly connected and functioning. Evidently, there was no sound because the choir was making no sound. He found himself thinking about Joe's little performance the last evening. The picture of the silent choir faded. Across the black screen travelled a message in large yellow letters:

Make no mistake:
Merger is the greatest opportunity
of our generation.

Another followed it:

Independence is poverty.
Unification is prosperity.
Vote 'YES' for the merger
With the Oceanic Union.

A third and final message followed:

Vote Departmental preference
Vote Yes
Protect your NLG
Vote YES
Love your Department
VOTE YES

The screen turned momentarily blank, then, switched to the normal Departmental Logo screensaver. Taking a pile of Travel Permit applications from his in tray, Greg removed the manual stamp from his right-hand desk draw, inked and dated it, then, began stamping the applications. Neither he nor the other 199 Operatives on the floor commented.

Later that morning, just as he was beginning to think about his morning spliff break, Greg looked up to see the young woman who had referred to herself as Tick sauntering her way down the aisle. He could not avoid noticing how low cut her dress was, nor the fact that she wore no bra. Her breasts were swinging in time with her hips. Greg became aware that she was walking directly towards his workstation. He immediately averted his eyes, not wishing to be accused of sexual harassment. As she came to a halt immediately beside his desk, Greg could see she carried a clipboard. "Hello, again, Co-Worker!" she said in her irritatingly cheerful voice. "Remember me? I'm your Vote." And with that she opened her arms wide and twirled round on the spot at a speed sufficient to force her breasts outwards against the material of her dress and raise her skirt. Greg was afforded a brief view of her white knickers. She beamed her engaging smile directly at him. "Have you decided how to cast me yet, Co-Worker?"

Greg didn't answer. He was finding it rather difficult to concentrate on anything other than the woman's entirely Compliant body shape and her abnormally revealing costume. Before he had time to think of a response, she had pulled back his wheeled chair and sat promptly down on his lap. Had he not already been silent, Greg would most certainly have been rendered totally speechless. "Is there anything you'd like to ask about this terribly important matter before you cast me?" asked the woman in apparent seriousness. "Is there any little thing you would like me to help you with?" Her enormous eyelashes blinked slowly up and down. "Anything you would like me to say or do in order to help you arrive at the decision to vote 'yes'?" This last was said as she ran her thumb and index finger of her right hand up and down his tie.

Greg was beginning to perspire. He was also having some difficulty breathing. He looked at his Co-Workers seated at the workstations closest to him. None of them appeared to notice anything unusual, all seemingly absorbed in their work. Now, the woman was beginning to run her fingers of her left hand through his hair. "You have such Compliant eyes, Co-Worker," she whispered breathlessly. "And I have to say I'm quite overcome with your obvious Departmental Commitment. Is there anything, anything at all, I can do to help you in your decision to vote for the merger?" She whispered this last directly into his ear as she squirmed on his lap. Greg shut his eyes, partly in profound embarrassment, partly in a wholly different kind of response.

He would have said it was a mere few seconds later that he opened them. But the woman was gone from his lap. In fact, she was nowhere to be seen. The bell for spliff break rang. All 200 staff on the floor rose from their stations and made rapidly for the staff rest facility.

The remainder of the day proceeded normally and Greg caught the boat from the 1st floor window back to the jetty as if he had done the same thing every day of his working life.

Arriving at home, Greg was about to press his palm against the door lock when the door slid open anyway. Joe danced excitedly around him with a box on his head, on which he had coloured an image that Greg took to be a fish head. Though obviously highly animated, no sound was coming from inside. Greg gently lifted the box off his son's shoulders to reveal a perfectly normal Joe – normal that was apart from the silence. The boy was once again opening and closing his mouth wordlessly. Eventually, he said, "Hi, Pop. I'm being a Gill-Breather. I know all about them. There's Fishpersons and Sharkmen an'… an… an' everything! Gill-Breathers are amazing!"

Greg looked past his son to the Nutriprep area where Grete was coordinating the evening nutrition. The Departmental Nutritional Instruction Manual was open at the first choice for that day's entries. She smiled at her husband. "He's been like this since he got home from EdFac. At least it's been quiet!" Still uneasy, but relieved to find relative normality at home, Greg walked over to his wife in the Nutriprep and kissed her lightly on the cheek. "We're running a bit behind," she said. "The voting site was slow and I had to wait. Did you cast your vote at work?"

Greg thought back to the young woman with the red tick and felt extreme embarrassment. He was hardly going to be able to explain the day's events in a way Grete could understand. He simply answered, "No, I didn't know we could yet."

"Oh, yes," said Grete enthusiastically. "There's information up all over the screens. Voting finishes tomorrow night. You'll have to get your overdrive engaged, sweet Co-Worker."

"And you've been following the campaigns?" Greg asked, becoming more interested.

"Absolutely!" Grete confirmed.

Greg thought carefully before asking his next question. "So, err, what would you say are the main arguments for and against the merger?"

Grete put down her nutricombiner carefully. It was the NutriDep 2.11v. They'd thought carefully about the cost before committing. But it was a huge advance over the 2.11t and it came with a level 5 recommendation from the Department. "Now, why would you ask that, sweet Co-Worker? The Department is quite clear in all the DepCasts. This is a once-in-a-generation opportunity to improve the lives of the whole Republic."

"Oh, sure," he replied cautiously. "I know that. I was just wondering if you'd looked into the arguments of the 'Vote No' campaign."

Grete thought for a moment, frowning. "I'm not sure there is one," she replied. "I've seen only what the Department has issued in the DepCasts." She hesitated. "At least, that is, I'm sure there is a 'No' campaign. After all, we live in the finest democracy in the world. The Department invented bureaucratic democracy. Yes, that's it. There will definitely be a 'Vote No' campaign. It's just I'm not interested. The Department has said how we should cast our votes. To do anything else would be far too dangerous."

Later, when Joe was asleep in his Partition, Grete had gone out to SocEngage, leaving Greg alone in the LivUnit. He sat down on the sofa in front of the SkypeWAll. It glowed a faint light green, awaiting his instruction. "List 'Vote Yes' Campaign sites," he instructed. The sites began appearing on the WAll in 20-point Departmental Typeface, starting from top left and filling the screen progressively towards the bottom right. At the top of the screen flashed a message "Over 20 million sites. Go to Page 2?" He opened the 1st site at the top left corner of the WAll. Instantly, the whole wall lit up in a cacophony of brightly coloured moving images and loud music. Greg hit the mute button for fear of waking Joe.

He watched in fascination as marching bands, bunting and balloons filled the screen. Eventually, all the images faded to one of beautiful young people of both sexes. All were dressed in the same referendum uniform of revealing white clothing adorned with big red ticks. All had long flowing blond hair and ran happily hand in hand over green fields, waving in excitement towards the ocean. As the programme neared its end, the camera focussed on a young man and a young woman standing on a cliff looking down at the ocean. The SkypeWAll around them softened to a haze as they turned to face the camera. The young woman was smiling but crying tears of evident happiness. She and the young man looked lovingly at each other and nodded. Then, they embraced in a passionate kiss. A caption rose behind them: "Vote Yes for happiness." Greg noted the site counter at the top right side of the WAll. It stood just a little short of 100 million page views.

"List 'Vote No' Campaign sites," He instructed, and waited. Then, he continued to wait. Normally, this only happened when a site was heavily engaged. Greg wondered if a huge number of people were looking at the 'Vote No' campaigns and considering voting against Departmental Recommendation. He smiled wryly. "That would be an interest event," he thought. Over a minute had passed and Greg was just about to give up when a single site reference appeared in the top left of the WAll. "Open," Greg instructed. The screen turned to grey, like the colour of the sky on a rainy day. In the middle of the WAll in a slightly darker grey 12-point typeface that Greg did not recognise, a short message appeared. Greg squinted to see what it said. Eventually, he read "Vote no." Below it was a small black cross. Once again, Greg looked up to the site counter at the top right hand corner of the WAll. As he watched, it clicked over from 004 to 005.

IV

As he sat on the LivUnit doorstep, Greg's mind ran over the Departmental Manual for Daily Living. He had learned DaLiv by heart in year 3 at EdFac like everyone else and contentiously rote learned each update within 24 hours of its release. But he could recall no instructions or advice that covered this situation. As the minutes ticked away towards Curfew, he began to hope his father was just punishing him, teaching him a lesson by scaring him. But with each passing minute his hope of the door being opened diminished. Greg looked around at his possessions – few enough, but more than he could carry, nevertheless. He moved the various boxes and carrier bags to the side of the step. Shouldering his satchel that contained his tablet, he picked up one suitcase. Then, he stepped down into the street. Out of habit, he turned right towards the Suburbia Transport Link. Arriving at the edge of the Suburbia Terminal Plaza, he hesitated. He had lodged no Intention of Absence with SocEngage. His i-Comm carried no SocPermit and he was nowhere that one might normally lawfully Engage, anyway. "Only two categories are unlawfully present in public places after Curfew," he found himself quoting from the Manual, "vagrants and terrorists." The light was falling fast now and he began to feel genuinely uneasy. The quote finished itself in his mind without his bidding, "and both may lawfully be Retired on sight by an Authorised Agent of the Department."

As he debated his painfully inadequate options, coming from behind him, Greg heard the one sound he least wished to hear. A melody was wafting over the twilight air towards him; a melody he knew well; a melody that froze his muscles and made him hold his breath. "If you ever hear Für Elise played," his father had told him, "stop what you're doing and put down what you're holding. Then, just wait to be told what to do." Later, the same instruction had been given at EdFac. They had practised it in the Playspace and everyone had stopped and dropped what they were holding. They had thought it was fun. But he had only seen the true meaning of the message when out walking with his father at the age of 7 years 4 months and 15 days. They were at a children's SocEngage in the PlayPark. Then, just like now, the tune had come to them from a distance. He had watched as all around him adults looked up fearfully. Then, his father had torn some toy he was holding from his hand and thrown it on the ground along with a bag he himself had been holding. His father stood, feet apart with his arms out, his fingers spread and his palms facing backwards, his satchel still swaying from his shoulder. He had hissed a whisper to his son to do the same. Greg Complied and watched every other adult around him do exactly the same, mimicked by the children. As the sound grew louder, he had felt a rumbling motion through the ground accompanied by a foul stench. It was to be some years before he could name it as fossil fuel. He had not dared turn or move. Then, some distance away to his right a man had quite suddenly started running away from them. From behind him, from outside his field of vision, a plume of flame leapt forward engulfing the man, who did not have time even to scream. He burned where he stood, his fired flesh adding to the stench in the air. Greg had been frightened, more frightened than he had ever felt before. Then, without warning, the vibration had ceased, the smell receded and the tune died away. Later, thinking about the event at home, what had terrified him most was that everyone had then continued behaving exactly as they had been doing, simply ignoring the charred remnants of the dead man smoking in an unrecognisable melted heap of flesh and bone and clothing. Worst of all, his father had simply refused to discuss the subject.

Now, it was happening again, though this time, Greg was quite alone in the plaza. At the sound of the Für Elise melody, he stopped instantly, conditioned by his childhood experience. Then, he put down his case and stood quite still. The low guttural rumble of a heavy vehicle's fossil-fuelled engine told of its slow, ponderous approach towards him across the Plaza, the music growing louder. Afraid to turn, he stood dead still. No

Departmental instruction covered such a situation, because this did not happen to Co-Workers. In the fading twilight, a pool of bright light from the vehicle's spotlight bar flowed forward like some viscous liquid around his feet. Greg watched his own shadow split the growing pool of light on the ground in front of him as it crept forward on the slow approach of the large vehicle.

The machine stopped. Greg could feel the vibration of its idling engine through the ground no more than a couple of metres behind him. He could smell its noxious, antiquated exhaust fumes. A loudspeaker crackled.

"Stop," said a voice superfluously over a loudspeaker. "Do not move. Drop your satchel. Reveal any weapons slowly and place them on the ground in front of you. If you attempt any form of violence we will Retire you without further warning."

The voice was dark and metallic, the antithesis of human. Greg Complied, his feet motionless, his body shaking.

"Remove your clothing starting with your jacket and shirt. Make no fast movements."

Greg's teeth began to chatter. With shaking hands, he unzipped his jacket and began to remove it, followed by his shirt.

"No sudden movements," the loudspeaker reminded him. "Now, your lower garments."

Greg unfastened his belt, allowing his trousers to fall to his feet. He began to lift his right foot in order to step out of them when the voice interjected sharply. "You have not been instructed to reposition. Do not reposition unless instructed." A moment's silence followed then, "Remove all clothing," said the voice.

As Greg's hands slid his underpants down his legs, he discovered he had wet himself. Finally, he stood naked. "Raise your arms to 45^0 below horizontal," instructed the voice. "Spread your fingers apart, palms facing behind you." Greg Complied instantly as the sun began to drop behind the Transport Link Terminal.

"Reposition and turn," said the voice.

Greg stepped from the bunched trousers at his feet and turned round.

He was confronted with the sight of a matt black angular vehicle, the size of a small refuse cleanser. But this was no sanitation vehicle. Its front window slits were protected with a mesh screen, its wheels covered with protectors. A long barrelled-gun protruded prominently at the top and was pointing directly at him.

"Lower your head," instructed the voice. He Complied instantly. A laser scanned him slowly from foot to head, pausing for several seconds at the embedded barcode on his forehead.

"Gregor Workman, 4978," read the voice from some screen deep inside the vehicle, "Suburbia sector 88, LivUnit 915689734. Is this you?"

Greg nodded, his voice failing him.

"Is this you?" the voice demanded louder.

"Yes, yes, it's me, Greg Workman, 4978-88-915689734," he yelled back in genuine terror.

"You are not registered as a permitted presence in this public place at this prohibited time. Why are you here? Are you a terrorist? Are you a vagrant? On your knees, now." The last word was shouted, almost spat out.

Greg dropped where he stood, the belt buckle from his trousers penetrating his right knee. He did not notice the pain. He did not notice that he had involuntarily defecated.

"No! No! I'm a Co-Worker. You can check with my parents. They've thrown me out. I've got nowhere to go."

"Then you are a vagrant, former Co-Worker Greg Workman 4978-88-915689734. Retirement will follow in 15 seconds."

"No please, no! You don't understand. They don't mean it. It's just to scare me." Greg had his arms extended in front of him and his palms raised in an instinctive gesture of self-protection. He glanced behind him at the setting sun. "Look, it's not quite Curfew yet. It's not illegal to be out yet. I'm sure I can get home in time if you let me go. Please. Please, let me go."

The voice was silent for a moment. "We have checked with Central. You are authorised to attempt to reach your LivUnit by Curfew, Co-Worker. We will follow. If you do not reach your LivUnit by Curfew or if the LivUnit does not admit you, you will be Retired. Leave now. You have 2 minutes 58 seconds. You will be followed."

Picking up only his satchel, Greg turned towards the LivUnit and, by virtue of adrenalin, ran faster than he knew he was capable of running. He arrived on the doorstep, fell to his knees and slammed his palm repeatedly on the lock. The door slid back soundlessly in its normal fashion. Behind him in the street, the headlights of the Neighbourhood Watch's armoured car lit up two bright pools on the street, while its searchlights turned the doorstep area to near daylight. The searchlights remained trained on the door for a few moments after it closed.

Greg entered with 4 seconds to spare.

V

Greg woke in front of the SkypeWAll. Checking his i-Comm, he found it was his normal rising time and that he had spent the night on the sofa.

"Good morning, sleepy Co-Worker!" called Grete from the Nutriprep area. "You were so soundly asleep when I got home, I thought I'd leave you." She pecked him lightly on the cheek as he joined her. She was dressed in her MedFac mustard coloured, one-piece uniform. Despite her long black hair being tied into a severe bun, Greg thought she still managed to look wonderful. She had kept her figure well since they had signed their 1st Contract. He had no doubt she could still get into the Contract Ceremonial Suit if she wished to, which was more than he could ever hope to do. Sometimes, he would look from their primary Ceremony hologram to his wife and back again. He loved her as much now as he had then and could detect no appreciable difference in her appearance in the 15 years that had passed. She ranked higher in his life than his work for the Department (something that he would never admit to in the wrong circles) and he often wondered how he had managed to get so lucky after making such a bad start to his adult life. Grete handed him an opened container of freshly hydrated NutriFluid. He tipped his head back and drank.

"Same flavour as last week?" he queried.

"Joe loves it," she replied. "He'd drink twice his daily allocation if I let him."

"The Department is happy you are satisfied with your purchase. Be happy, too!" he quoted.

She giggled and kissed him. "You'd better go cleanse, or you'll be late. And don't forget. Today is your last opportunity to vote. Don't come home without voting for the merger, Co-Worker!" Greg knew she was teasing but somehow still felt uneasy.

Arriving at work in the same manner as on the previous day, all around him seem to have forgotten entirely that a mere 48 hours previously the water had been safely contained in the river. Greg stepped out of the boat and passed through security without comment. Sitting at his workstation, his 1st act was to switch on his screen. Instead of the normal Departmental aphorism to '*work productively, work happily*', the screen was immediately filled with the same dancing 20-somethings in white clothing and red ticks as had appeared on the SkypeWAll the previous evening. Reminded of his wife's admonition to vote, he switched to the polling station site and pressed his thumb to the Identiscan. 'Welcome, Co-Worker, Greg Workman 4978-88-915689734,' the screen responded. 'Do you wish to cast your vote? You have only until 17.00 hours to do so.' Greg thought back to Tick's words, "I'm a vote. You can cast me," she had said suggestively while looking deep into his eyes and squirming on his lap.

Greg felt immediately guilty. "Not just yet," he found himself saying to the screen. "I'm not quite decided." Without response, the Polling Station site faded away in favour of Greg's overnight e-mails. The 1st was a round robin ("What's a Robin?" Greg always wondered) from the Lev6 section manager in Personnel on the floor above. It advised all staff that as soon as the referendum was over and the majority of Co-Workers had voted for the merger, the Department was expecting a delegation of guest Operatives from the Oceanic Union who were tasked with responsibility for standardising Permit Section procedures with those in use in the OU.

"If these folk really are gill-breathers as Joe says," he found himself thinking, "how are they going to breathe our air, never mind use our equipment? This merger is weird. They have their lives and procedures and we have ours. We have absolutely nothing in common. How are we supposed to merge?" As he pondered matters above his pay grade, Greg heard a noise coming from the landing at the far end of the floor behind him. He turned to see the double doors thrown open and a group of 11 young vote-people dressed in the usual white and red uniform, heading his way, blowing multi-coloured party horns and laughing and shouting at one another. The Posse, which included Tick, arrived at his desk giggling and breathless. As far as Greg could see, no other worker on the floor indicated interest or even suggested that they had noticed, despite the fact that the levitious little group was entirely impossible to ignore.

Greg looked up, hoping his expression was enough to convey how tiresome he was finding the intrusion. "Greetings, Co-Worker! Remember me?" said Tick as she sat down on his lap before he had time to object. Without warning, she threw her arms around his neck and wriggled around, pressing her mouth firmly against his in a passionate kiss. The rest of the group laughed helplessly while a young man proceed to record images with a Holocam. Finally, she released him and he pulled back sharply, pushing her away from him with both hands.

"What in the name of JeKAllah are you playing at, young woman?" he yelled.

"Now, steady on, Co-Worker," said the man with the Cam, stepping forward as they all suddenly became serious. "We've just come to help you cast your vote for the merger, that's all. If you'd been expeditious about it previously, we'd not need to be here at all."

Greg was immediately taken aback at the suggestion, he was anyway at fault, or to be blamed for the young woman's outrageous behaviour. "Well, if that's all you're here for," he found himself answering, "how about a bit of fair play 1st? How about I hear from someone in the 'Vote No' camp?" All the young people looked at him aghast. He might as well just have announced he was a suicide bomber.

Without a word, they gathered in a circle, arms about one another's shoulders, and conferred. After 57 seconds of this, the little huddle broke up. The same young man as before spoke again. "Co-Worker, are you aware that you are the last remaining voter in the whole of the Republic who has yet to cast your vote?" Greg was not aware. In fact, he was extremely surprised to hear this was the case and entirely doubted the veracity of the white-clothed speaker in front of him. However, he was not going to lose face by displaying potential ignorance to this young upstart who was clearly not old enough to have left EdFac yet, let alone gained any degrees. He simply continued looking at the young man without speaking.

"Very well, Co-Worker," continued the young man. "If a visit from the 'No' campaign is what you want, then, that is what you will get." And with that, the whole group turned back in the direction from which they had come. With a final flourish of their party horns, they pushed their way through the swing doors and were gone. Greg was more than relieved that there were no more interruptions, even from his e-mails, until spliff break.

When he reached his desk after the break, Greg noticed that the System had made a diary entry for him at noon, details not disclosed. He thought no more about such a routine event and worked on until the clock in the corner of his screen indicated he had just 90 seconds before the appointed time. Checking, he had actually managed to catch up with the schedule after the morning's interruptions, Greg stopped. He looked towards the swing doors at the near end of the floor and then, at those at the far end. Neither moved. He kept looking, then glancing back at the screen periodically. Finally, the left side door at the far end moved. He waited to see who would enter but no one did. Eventually, the door was pushed just a little wider but still no one entered. Greg was reminded uncomfortably of his own behaviour 15 years ago, on the 7th Floor. Finally, he could stand the suspense no longer. He stood up, checking to see if any Co-Workers around him were watching. All were seemingly absorbed in their own activities. Greg moved towards the doors in what he hoped was an unobtrusive manner. Arriving, he pushed one open and passed through. The sight that confronted him was the last thing he might have expected to see. In front of him stood a Vagrant. They were an almost extinct category since the Department had announced its Health and Safety Drive 11 months after his confrontation with Neighbourhood Watch 15 years ago. It was an event he had no wish to repeat. Simply being seen talking in the street to a person such as this could, with his earlier poor Departmental record, be devastating. He recoiled from the sorry individual standing before him. Ragged, dirty and smelling of every kind of uncleansed impurity, the man stood 150 centimetres tall. He leaned heavily on a cane he held in his right hand, and wheezed with the effort of breathing. He carried no satchel and looked well beyond Retirement age. Just as Greg was wondering how in the name of the Republic the man had managed to slip past security, the vagrant spoke.

"Greg Workman?" he asked with difficulty. "I'm the Area 'Vote No' Coordinator. How may I help you?"

Greg looked at the wheezing old Vagrant as if he had just announced he was the Permanent Secretary of the Department. "You are the Area 'Vote No' coordinator?" he repeated slowly.

The Vagrant made an enormous effort to speak again. "Co-Worker, if you force me to repeat everything I say, this consultation is going to take a very long time. There are 8,433,289 voters in this sector and I am working alone. What would it be like if everyone asked to see me, then, absorbed my time in unnecessary questions?" The man looked at him defiantly.

"I apologise, Co-Worker," he said immediately. "You're the 1st person from the 'No' campaign I've ever seen, let alone talked to."

"Vagrant," replied the man still looking defiant.

"Sorry?" asked Greg confused.

"There you go questioning me again, Co-Worker. I'm not a Co-Worker, I'm a Vagrant. I am Respected Vagrant Diversity 4989207."

Greg didn't dare question the man on his statement further, though he had not a clue what the terms and number the Vagrant was quoting actually meant.

"May I ask your name?" asked Greg, playing for time while he composed his thoughts.

The man looked at him with an expression somewhere between frustration and anger. "Don't be ridiculous, Co-Worker. You should know by now that Vagrants don't have names. But if the number's too long for your soft, over-pampered brain to remember, you can call me Div 498."

"Thank you," said Greg uncertainly, not noticing that his MathImplant had failed to cut in to remember the number for him. "But, err, if you're, err, Diverse, shouldn't you have been... you know, well, Retired at birth?"

The man paused as if deciding whether to reply. "My Diversity didn't develop until I was 15. And my parents were both Lev6ers. They bought Respected Status for me. Look. I've got a bar code, same as you, see." Div 498 pushed back the sleeve on his left arm. Sure enough, he had a bar code. Unlike Greg's embedded bar code, this man's was tattooed onto his wrist in old-fashioned black lines and numbers. "The Department respects Diversity," he continued. "That's why we're called 'Respected Diversities'. Any fool knows that. Where have you been all your life, Co-Worker?"

Greg didn't answer. He was beginning to wonder himself. "Anyway," continued Div, "none of this has anything to do with the 'Vote No' campaign. Why did you want to see me?"

Greg wasn't actually too sure himself, now, the No Campaign Regional Coordinator was actually standing in front of him. "Err, how about you tell me why I should vote no?"

"I should have thought that was obvious to you, Co-Worker. This union is weird, doomed from the start. The Oceanics have their lives and procedures and we have ours. They breathe through water, we breathe in the air. Nothing wrong with either. But we have absolutely nothing in common. To merge our lives and procedures successfully with gill-breathing Fishpersons, every Co-Worker, every Co-Educate would have to become a Gill-Breather themselves"

"I have to admit," said Greg, "I was thinking much the same only this morning."

"Of course, you were, Co-Worker," said Div 498, his tone softening a little.

"So… why does the Department want the Republic to become part of the Oceanic Union?"

Div 498 nodded upwards in the direction of the security cameras. Then he grabbed hold of Greg's arm and drew him close to himself as if he was about to whisper something. Then, thinking better of it, he let go of Greg's arm, turned, and wheezed his way slowly down the stairs, leaning on the bannister the whole way down.

Greg shook his head at the surrealism of the situation, then turned and pushed his way back through the double doors and returned to his workstation.

The clock on his screen was showing 15.37. "Vote," Greg reminded himself. "Don't forget to vote." But which way was he to vote? The Department wanted him to vote 'Yes'. Even by Departmental standards, phenomenal resource had been put into the 'Vote Yes' campaign. "But," Greg mused, "they have offered no plausible justification for doing something that on the face of it looks to be detrimental to the interests of our country. Yet, everyone is hugging and kissing me, telling me how good it's going to be for the Departmental Republic after the merger. If the Department believes that, why don't I? And why doesn't anyone else around me think like this? Perhaps, they do. Perhaps, they're just saying and doing what they're expected to. Perhaps, I should too. But what about Div 498?"

Round and round the thoughts went in Greg's head. For 15 years, he had done everything in his power to forget the past and Comply. "So, why," he wondered, "am I having such difficulty with this? The easiest thing to do would be to load the polling station page right now, vote yes and be done with it. No more silly, sexy kids, no more wheezing old men." He leaned forward to speak to the System. "Polling Station," he said. The screen in front of him flickered, then sprang to life.

Up came the words, 'Do you wish to vote?'

"Yes," said Greg.

'Scan bar code,' the screen read. Greg bent his head forward in the normal way for the laser to scan him.

'Co-Worker Gregor Workman 4978-88-915689734. Is this you?'

Greg had hated hearing the question ever since his run in with Neighbourhood Watch. But he said "Yes" all the same.

'Press Identiscan,' read the words on the screen. Greg duly Complied.

'Scan Bar Code,' Greg read on the screen again. He frowned. But he knew full well there was no point in arguing with the System. As far as the System was concerned, the System was always right. Greg bent his head once again to let the laser scan him.

'Co-Worker, Gregor Workman 4978-88-915689734. Is this you?'

"Yes," Greg replied, a little more emphatically than was necessary.

'Press Identiscan,' read the words on the screen. Greg groaned. This didn't happen often. In fact, no one would ever admit to it happening at all. Ever. He assumed the Polling Station connection was overloaded. He knew the only solution was to wait. He would leave it until later. He still had until 17.00 hours to vote. And perhaps, by then, he would feel more able to make up his mind. Greg switched back to the Travel Permit Authorisations screen and proceeded with his work.

When he next looked at the clock, it was 16.49. He drew in his breath sharply. Still not sure which way he would cast his vote, he turned to the Polling Station site once again. The screen came up in the normal way. 'There is a 10-minute wait for this facility,' read the words on the screen. 'Do you wish to wait?' He had no option. As the offensive young man had pointed out, he might not be expeditious, but to fail to vote was unthinkable. He sat, tapping his fingers and tapping his foot in time to the clock counting down the waiting time second by second.

Finally, at 16.59.17, the letters on the screen morphed from the 10-minute wait message to the 'scan embedded barcode' message. Once again, Greg Complied.

Gregor Workman 4978-88-915689734. Is this you?
16.59.25. "Yes," replied Greg.
16.59.34. 'Press Identiscan,' said the words on the screen.
16.59.37. Greg Complied.
16.59.44. The Identiscan flashed.
16.59.51 'Do you wish to vote?' said the words on the screen.
16.59.53 "Yes," said Greg.
16.59.56 'Press the 'Yes' button to vote for the merger,' said the screen.
16.59.58. Greg reached towards the 'yes' and 'no' buttons on the screen.
16.59.59 Greg hesitated.
17.00.00. 'Poll Closed,' said the screen.

VI

Greg's parents had been in front of the SkypeWAll when he had burst into the LivUnit. Preoccupied with series 29 episode 143 of Protector of the Republic, they hadn't even noticed him enter. As the door slid soundlessly closed behind him, Greg had bent forward, leaning his hands on his knees and lowering his head, gasping for breath after breath. Here he had stood, unacknowledged by his parents for 3 full minutes. Then, with his heart rate slowly returning to normal, he had walked to his Partition and stepped into the Nanocleanse. He had never been so grateful for a cleansing in his entire life. To his amazement, the following morning, his parents had behaved as if nothing had happened. He had fallen gratefully into line with the mutual self-deception.

Some weeks later, when he was beginning to think life was finally returning to normal, Greg had woken on an 8th day and wondered what to do with the time off. Worshipers of JeKAllah used it for Mosque or 'Gogue or Church. But Greg's family had never been religious and he couldn't bring himself to believe the old Holy Manual myth that God rested from making the world on the 8th day. He was, nevertheless, grateful for the time off. For want of anything better to do, he had decided to visit the AmaBay Mall. With the sun shining brightly, he had shunned the Uber that was hovering hopefully outside and strode off in the direction of the park. It had still been early when he arrived and the Uber ranks had been largely empty. Kids on litter duty had been scouring the vast empty lot in search of their quota. Greg smiled at one, a girl of 9 years 3.5 months of age, as she scooted past on her skateboard, yellow contaminated waste bag in her hand. "Got any litter, Co-Worker?" she had asked as she shot by. Greg was about to say no, then thought better of it. He remembered litter duty well.

"What's your name?" he had asked.

The girl had pulled up her skateboard sharply about 3 metres from him.

"Trish Abdullah-Goldstein," she had answered without hesitating.

"How long have you been on duty, Trish Abdullah-Goldstein?" Greg had asked.

Trish had hesitated. "Are you Neighbourhood Watch?" she had asked, looking at him suspiciously.

Greg had smiled. "No, nothing like that. I just remember the time when I had to do what you're doing. I know how hard it is to make quota when the big kids steal the waste from you to meet their own targets."

Trish had seemed satisfied with his answer. "This is day 3," she said, unable to hide the sadness in her voice. Greg had been aware it would have started as a 4-hour shift. No more needed to be said.

"Have you, Co-Worker?" she had repeated. "Have you got any litter?"

Instead of answering, Greg had pushed his hands into his pockets in search of something to give the girl. In his back trouser pocket his left hand had touched his notebook. "Hardly litter," he had thought. He had already filled almost every page in closely written notes. When full, he would place the notebook back on the shelf in his partition awaiting the day when... well, Greg didn't really know what he would do with the notes. But nevertheless, something drove him on to record his thoughts and observations. But then, he had looked back at Trish Abdullah-Goldstein, who would no doubt prefer to spend the day at Mosque or 'Gogue or Church, worshiping JeKAllah, than here collecting litter on her skate board. She had looked tired. He had taken out the notebook.

"How many pieces short of quota are you?"

"24."

"If I give you three sheets of paper, you can tear each one into 4 parts. That's half what you're short of."

Trish had looked over each shoulder in turn, then up at the surveillance cam on the high pole in the corner of the huge Ubertaxi rank. Given that they were virtually alone in the rank, unsurprisingly, the camera had been pointing down at them. The camera's focus had moved as Trish watched.

"Not allowed," she had said, turning back to Greg. "Neighbourhood Watch make you start again when you do that."

"But if I tear them up before giving you the pieces?"

"Can't give 'em to me," Trish had said, nodding up towards the cam.

"Ah, yes, I have to drop them so you can pick them up."

Trish had nodded.

"And that means… I get fined a Thaler for each one I drop?"

Trish had nodded, solemnly.

"And you get paid…?"

"10 cents."

"Ah," Greg had said.

"Less income tax," Trish had replied.

"Ahh," he had said.

"Less National Insurance," Trish had added.

"Ahhh," Greg had said.

"Less University Accumulation Fund," Trish had continued.

"Ahhhh," he had said, sounding like he was seeing a Medic at MedFac.

"Less…"

"OK, I get the holo," Greg had said. "How much do you take to LivUnit for each piece of litter you pick up?"

Trish had looked at him suspiciously. "Are you sure you're not Neighbourhood Watch?" she asked.

"Definitely not," Greg had replied.

"Not National Revenue Service?"

"Not that either," Greg had reassured her.

"Not Child Vagrancy Suppression?"

"Definitely not that one."

Trish held up 3 fingers. Greg had nodded his understanding. Then, she folded one finger at the knuckle. Greg nodded again.

"So, if I drop 12 pieces of paper, I get fined…"

"12 Thalers," the girl had finished for him.

"And you get paid…"

"36 cents."

"You're good at maths, aren't you?" Greg had commented. "Have you had your MathImplant already?"

Trish had shaken her head, then said, "Look are you going to drop this litter or not, Co-Worker? Cos if not, I've got a quota to make and time is money."

Greg had thought that if Trish had been born 100 years previously, she would have made a fine entrepreneur. But he had not voiced his thought. Instead, opening his precious notebook and wondering how he had got into this situation in the 1st place, he had carefully had counted out 3 sheets of his precious paper and had torn each sheet into 4 pieces. Then, he had looked at the cam which was now trained on the main entrance to the Mall and back to Trish. With a sigh, he had bent down and dropped the pile of 12 pieces of paper neatly onto the ground from a height of 3 centimetres. He had stepped back. His i-Comm had made a 'ping' sound as his credit account told it that his balance had just been reduced by 12 Thalers.

Without saying any more, Trish had jumped forward from her skateboard and retrieved the little pile before it blew away. She stepped back, then, 1st re-checking that the cam wasn't trained on them, she had looked Greg directly in the eye and torn all 12 sheets in half again before dropping them in her contamination sack and skating away, punching the air and yelling.

He had heard the 'ping' of a second message reaching his i-Comm. He had known it would be his credit account informing him of the debit of another 12 Thalers. Greg had groaned inwardly and recalculated his losses. He had just spent 24 Thalers (excluding the cost of the notebook pages), of which young Trish would be credited with 72 cents. The other T23.28 would be retained by the Department to offset the cost of the strongly worded letter he would now receive for littering. Any balance would be remitted directly into Treasury funds to support the provision of Co-Worker services. "And that, of course," Greg had found himself thinking, "was taxed money before I spent it. To take back to LivUnit T24 required I earn...'

T93.60 his MathImplant interjected.

"So, from T93.60 I got T24, Trish got C72 and the Department got T92.88. My Tax Thalers at work," he had thought, proceeding towards the Mall and wondering how much he could now afford to spend in the AmaBay that day.

Entering AmaBay Mall 14, Greg had been confronted with a HolloSkype of a young woman singing 'I am H-A-P-P-Y'. He had walked straight thorough her without hesitating and made for the elevator bank. Greg had no interest in the cosmetics and perfumes that filled floors 1-7, or SocEngage 4 on floor 8, nor for that matter, Nutri on floors 15-23, or LivUnit big-ticket goods, floors 24-38. Years ago, he would have stopped at Bodyfit, floors 39-51, but he had long outgrown that. He had taken the lift that was heading to the top floors, 91-93, cigs and spliffs. Here he exited the lift, climbed a further 3 floors past admin and finance and finally, reached the roof exit when the antiques and bric-a-brac shacks were housed. Since the Department did not strictly approve of the traders, everyone visiting the roof shacks had their holo taken on the way in and the way out. Greg had been wary when he 1st visited the place with teenage friends, daring and egging one another on. But when others had lost interest, having found nothing of deviant significance, he had continued to visit, fascinated by the artefacts of pre-Departmental culture.

Greg had emerged into the bright sunlight of the roof terrace of AmaBay Mall 14, floor 97. A three metre Plexiglas screen had been added all the way round the building in 2097, just after, it was rumoured, the 97th jumper had descended to the ground by the fastest route possible. He had never known if the rumour was true, but had had to admit it had a certain sense of Departmental Symmetry about it. Greg had looked around him at the old familiar scene. He had been coming here since he was what? 12 years old? He loved the makeshift stalls, tarpaulins flapping in the breeze, the wooden trestle tables (yes, real wood, some of them, Greg reminded himself) the ancient plastic and cardboard boxes with their even more ancient contents. The roof terrace was divided into sectors – electronics, video & audio, books (physical), furniture, toys, mechanical and so on. In the centre stood the pride of the whole gathering – an antique mobile burger bar. It even had a blackboard and chalk menu with prices marked in old currency units. If you wanted to, you could buy coins from the coin collecting stalls and use them to pay at the bar. The only thing the bar did not have, of course, was real burgers. Health and Safety would never have given it a licence to sell animal protein. Instead, it sold the same Nutridrinks and substitutes as everywhere else did – but cleverly marketed them under the names of cheeseburger, hot dog, cat food and so on. "Obesity steals food from the mouths of your Co-Workers," Greg had thought in the words of the old Departmental health aphorism.

He had not been hungry. He had made his way to the book area, wandering the aisles between the stalls, inhaling the ancient atmosphere and watching the other Bookbugs elbow one another in search of the best purchases. "Morning, Co-Worker," a stallholder he knew slightly had called. "Got a nice copy of Harry Potter and the Non-Compliant Quaffle."

"No, thanks, Co-Worker," he had replied, "I've already got a signed 1st edition of the complete works of Albus Dumbledore at my LivUnit.

"Let me know if you ever want to sell them, Co-Worker. I pay top price."

Greg had smiled and nodded. He would never part with the Complete Works. Dumbledore was a giant of a novelist. His signature alone was priceless. Something had told Greg the trader would have difficulty in rising to a fair price. Instead, he had made his way towards the pre-Departmental Era stalls right out at the edge of the building next to the Plexiglas screen.

"Morning, Greg," called a familiar voice. "How's my favourite young Co-Worker?"

Greg had giggled. The woman addressing him was one Gee Robinson, 57 years 4 months 11 days of age. Almost old enough to be his mother, but not too old to be making suggestive remarks to him. She had fluttered her eyelids at him and giggled back. "Blessed to be a Departmental Co-Worker, thank you," he had replied in the standard response. "How's my favourite antiquarian book dealer?" Gee had gestured a double thumbs up. "Anything new in?" he asked.

"You can look in that box over there," Gee had said. "Not had time to sort it yet."

Greg had looked in the direction she nodded to see a large plastic box standing on a wooden trestle table. He walked directly to it before anyone else got there.

"Inevitable," thought Greg. "Mostly trash." He had picked up a torn copy of 'If on a Winter's Night A Co-Worker' and inspected it disdainfully. There was a lot of so-called pre-Departmental literature about. But when the title included something Departmentally inspired, you had to treat it with a pinch of Nutriflavouring. He had placed it respectfully back in the box, not wishing to damage it any further, even if it was valueless. Then he had rummaged around a little more, bringing up two volumes at once that were both in fair condition. He had held the two books out in front of him, one in each hand. Both had captivated his attention, but each for different reasons.

In his left hand, he had held a book by Franz Kafka, an author he knew well. At home, he had a copy of Metamorphosis Reversed. He had much enjoyed the inspiring story of how Departmental Medic Grete Samsa had laboured day and night to find a cure for her husband's illness and how the Department had lavished budgetary credit and support staff on her as she performed her Departmentally inspired miracles. He knew it was childish, but he did so enjoy the fact that he shared a name with the protagonist's husband.

But this book, this was different. 1ˢᵗly, he had not known the title. It was called Der Prozess. Greg frowned at the word. He could never remember seeing it before. 2ⁿᵈly, it was in a language he had never read before. But strangest of all to Greg was that there was something wrong with the date and age of the book. Kafka had published Metamorphosis Reversed in 2043, eight years after the establishment of the Departmental Republic. But this book had a date inside the cover of 1925. Clearly there was a mistake. Kafka couldn't have written two books so far apart. People didn't live that long in those days. He wondered if maybe there were two Franz

Kafka's. "Unlikely," he had thought, "unless maybe they were grandfather and grandson." He had evaluated it a little longer. 'Might be something to do with Prozac,' he had mused, looking at the title again. "No use to me, though," he thought, putting it back in the box.

The other had been equally odd. 'George Orwell' was a name he knew well. And this time there was no issue over the date. Orwell had written 1984 as a pre-Departmental Republic manifesto in the year 1984. Everyone knew that. It was taught in Primary EdFac history. That's why it was called 1984. And indeed, this book had the date '1984' in the publication details on the 3rd page. But it still wasn't right. The title was spelt out in letters – 'Nineteen Eighty-Four.' Greg wondered if it was a special edition. He had smiled and turned to his favourite scene, the last page, with Winston Smith sitting outside the Chestnut Tree Café, tears of joy running down his face for the fact that the Ministry of Love had brought him and Julia together in lifelong union. Every time he read the scene it made him load up the Departmental Happy in Compliant Love page and look for a partner. And then, there was that outstanding last line. 'He loved Big Brother.' What more could a Co-Worker hope for, he had often mused, than to live a useful life, love a Co-Partner and love the Department he served? He was a sucker for 1984 – or Nineteen Eighty-Four as this edition had it. He had clutched the book a little tighter and turned back to Gee Robinson. "How much for this, Gee?" Greg had asked. Gee took the book from his hand and evaluated it.

"30 Thalers, Co-Worker?" The flirting had suddenly ceased. She had become all businesswoman. Greg had eyed her disdainfully without speaking. "20?" she asked hopefully. He still didn't respond. "All right, 15 and I'll give you any other book in the unsorted box you like, for nothing." Greg smiled. Without further thought, he had picked up the Kafka volume and held out his wrist for Gee to scan the embedded code. She had taken his hand as if to steady it for the laser, but held onto it rather longer than she really needed. "Any plans for later, Co-Worker?" she had asked. The fluttering eyelids were suddenly back.

"Yes," Greg had answered, "I have a date." Gee dropped his hand, a look of disappointment spreading across her face. "With George Orwell," he had said, smiling. "But my heart is already yours, Co-Worker," he had said, crossing his arms on his chest, one book still in each hand. "See you next week!"

VII

Greg had but moments to look at the screen flashing 'Poll Closed', before the 5.00 pm shutdown of the system. Co-Workers all around him were packing up and making for the boats. He had little option but to do the same. He wondered how he would explain to Grete that he had not voted. She would surely ask. Later, as he entered the LivUnit, she looked up from the Nutriprep area. She immediately put aside the meal preparations and walked straight up to him with a very straight face. Standing just centimetres in front of him, she said in a serious tone, "Gregor Workman 4978-88-915689734. Is this you?" Greg shook involuntarily. Inside his head the words resonated back 1st to his failure to vote that afternoon and then mixed with images of the twilight confrontation with the Neighbourhood Watch armoured vehicle on the plaza 15 years prior.

Greg looked at her aghast. His wife. His beautiful Co-Partner... asking... this. Could she know already, he had failed to vote? Could she be announcing the end of their Contract over the matter? Greg nevertheless composed himself and gave the standard procedural answer. "Yes, this is me."

For a moment, she simply looked at him, her face a study in seriousness. It was a moment as short as the one he had spent staring at those fateful words on his screen. 'Poll Closed'; a moment as long as the one during which Neighbourhood Watch decided on his fate. Then, she broke into a huge smile and flung her arms round him. "I'm so proud of you!" she cried out. In total confusion, he let her hug him, having not the slightest hint of what she could be referring to. Eventually, she pulled back a little and gave him a long deep kiss. Greg kissed her back, wondering what in the name of

JeKAllah he might have done to engender such a response from her. There was no Departmental Vacation Day. It was not their Contract Anniversary. It wasn't even Joe's birthday. Finally, in bemusement he pulled back a little and looked into her shining eyes. It reminded him of why he had Contracted with her in the 1st place; why they had renewed on Anniversary 7.

"This is nice," he said, smiling back at her. "But, err, what have I done to deserve such a welcome?"

"Now, don't give me that," said Grete. "You've been on the DepCasts hourly since I came home. You, Sweet Co-Worker, were the last person to vote. They're even saying that you consulted both sides of the argument and made up your own mind in favour of the Yes Vote." She stood back, smiling at him, tears in her eyes. "I'm so proud of you," she repeated. "*And* there was a full turnout – every single Co-Worker voted – *and* there has been a unanimous vote for the merger. Wo-hoh!" At this, she took him in a ballroom pose and danced him round the room. "We're going to become part of the Oceanic Union. We might even have Fishpersons for neighbours!"

Later that night, Greg lay awake while his happy Co-Partner slept in his arms. After Family Nutrition and when Joe had withdrawn to his Partition, she had gone on line and successfully applied for an Intimacy Permit. When the approval had come back immediately, Greg had refrained from articulating his surprise at the speed of response. They had withdrawn to their Partition immediately to execute the Permit. She had taken the lead in a way that reminded him of the 1st days of their relationship. It was a style of intimacy that had later evaded them. Whatever the cause, Greg was more than grateful. Nevertheless, despite the warm glow, he could not sleep. Listening silently to Grete's contented breathing, the questions flowed through his mind in rapid succession. Why had the Department chosen to mention him on the news bulletins?

How had they managed to make such a fundamental error over his voting? Who was the Respected Vagrant that had gained access to the Permits Building despite the security screens? And, most important of all, with the coming merger with the Oceanic Union, what did the future hold?

Finally, he fell into a disturbed sleep in which a Neighbourhood Watch vehicle circled him menacingly while he pondered his voting intention until the beautiful 'Vote Yes' girl sat on the lap of the Respected Vagrant and kissed him deeply. The next thing he was aware of was a bright shaft of Departmentally provided sunlight creeping steadily across the duvet and warming his face. 'Morning has broken like the 1st morning,' as the old Departmental folksong ran. "Praise for the singing, praise for the morning, praise the Department, joy of the world," hummed Greg as he stepped into the Nanocleanse.

Life proceeded uneventfully for several days after the referendum. Greg commuted to work, habitually checking the time on his i-Comm in his normal manner and catching the boat from near the City Transporter Terminal as if he had always done so. From the way Co-Workers around him talked, life might as well always have been like this. There had so far been no visible change to routines at home or at work as a result of the merger. But on the 6th day morning after the referendum, he arrived to find an announcement on his screen.

The Oceanic Delegation (Permits Division) arriving Month 4 Day 1 will occupy Water Floor 1 of the Permits Building. Consultation on Systems Integration will commence upon arrival. Co-Workers are urged to volunteer for the Departmental Delegation to the Consultation. Preparatory Cluster Group meetings will commence immediately.

Greg was intrigued. Quite how the Department proposed to integrate the Permits Section systems with the underwater counterpart in the Oceanic Union for the moment escaped him. His mind cast back to the conversation he had had on the landing with Div 498 – "We have nothing in common," Div 498 had said. "We'd all have to become Gill-Breathers for it to work."

"No chance of that," Greg thought. However, his curiosity remained unabated. Competition for the Delegation would surely be stiff with many applicants. Nevertheless, he pressed the 'apply' button that was flashing on his screen. As he prepared to turn to the page concerning the day's work, he was astound to see the screen flash back immediately with the words 'Application Accepted. Close your Workstation. Proceed immediately to 3rd Floor. Your allocated seat is number 101.' An icy tsunami surged through his arteries and out to the extremities of his body. A trap? If so, he had sprung it himself as a result of that old enemy – his own curiosity. But it was too late to reconsider his options. The instruction was unambiguous. To fail to comply was out of the question. Having closed his workstation, he climbed slowly to the 3rd floor and stood in front of a pair of swing doors that exactly matched those on the landing below. Instinctively, his gaze rose to the doorframe, seeking the security cameras. There were none. He tried the door. It swung open at his touch. Greg stepped through.

He had been expecting to find himself in a corridor. In fact, the door opened onto a room that occupied the whole of the floor in much the same way as it did on his own floor below. At the far end, near the opposite set of doors, stood a circle of chairs around an electronic Whitescreen. Several of the seats were occupied and a young woman was standing in front of the screen. She looked familiar. When he realised it was Tick, and that she was still dressed in a white referendum uniform, Greg closed his eyes and fought an inclination to turn around and walk out. Now regretting his decision to apply for participation in the Consultation Delegation, he supressed his frustration and strode across the room, determined to make the best of what was supposed to be a significant career opportunity.

When Tick saw him, her face beamed an apparently spontaneous smile. She broke off what she was saying to the little group in midsentence and addressed Greg. "Greg Workman! This is definitely you! How wonderful you have decided to enhance the status of our humble little group by joining us." Then, to the group, "Cluster Group Members, let me introduce you to our very own celebrity, Co-Worker Gregor Workman 4978-88-915689734. As many of you will remember, Greg was featured on the National DepCasts last week as being the final Co-Worker to cast his vote for the merger, having considered at length the benefits that the merger brings. Fellow Cluster Group members, welcome Greg Workman!" And with this, Tick started clapping, whereupon the group rose to their feet and followed her lead. Greg endured, more than enjoyed the welcome. He took what was now the last vacant of 13 chairs. Noting it was numbered 101 and that it was adjacent to Tick's, Greg looked up expectantly at her. He tried not to notice how closely the short white uniform clung to her body. What he did notice, however, was several other male members of the group also apparently trying not to notice what he was trying not to notice. "Or perhaps," he thought to himself a little uncharitably, "they're trying not to be noticed noticing what I'm trying not to notice."

For her part, Tick seemed not to notice any of it. "For our 1st session, Co-Workers," she continued, "we are going to learn the Anthem of the Union we have just joined, so as to be able to use it to welcome our esteemed OU Co-Workers when they arrive next month. I will 1st demonstrate this, then I would like you to join in. Co-Worker Diane Blacksmith will accompany me on keyboard." It was at this point Greg noticed a music stand placed a little outside the group. A woman of 32 years 2 months and 3 days stood up and walked to the stand, taking out her i-Comm as she did so. Tick waited as Diane solemnly opened the i-Comm to the web page containing the music for the OU anthem, Greg presumed, and placed it onto the music stand. Then she looked at Tick, evidently waiting for instruction to commence the music. Tick stood in the centre of the circle of chairs, and stood to attention. It was immediately evident to all assembled that she was choking back emotion and taking enormous genuine pride in what she was doing. Greg began to hope that he might finally be about to learn something significant about this merger and the strange people who lived under the water, when Tick nodded to Diane. "Start," instructed Diane to the machine and nodded back to Tick, whereupon Tick began opening and closing her mouth. It took a couple of moments for Greg to realise he could not hear her singing anything. It took a couple more for him to realise that no music was coming from the i-Comm either. When the silent performance had continued for upwards of a minute, Tick ceased moving her mouth and nodded to Diane who instructed the machine to stop.

Tick turned to the group. "Co-Workers," she began, "I know many of you will have found the OU anthem as deeply moving as I did. We will take a 5-minute rest break for us all to recompose ourselves." Then she turned and walked out of the double doors.

"Incredible," said a voice to Greg's right.

Greg turned to see who was addressing him. A white haired male Co-Worker of 73 years and 4 days was looking at Greg with tears in his eyes. "What is?" asked Greg in genuine confusion.

"That anthem," said the elder Co-Worker. "I've never heard or seen anything so moving in my entire life. Blessed be the Department that I should remain unRetired long enough to see this day."

"Well said, Co-Worker," came a female voice to the older man's right.

"Aye, well said, Co-Worker," repeated the person to the woman's other side. And so the aphorism continued round the circle until it came to Greg's turn. All members of the group looked at him expectantly. Try as he might, Greg found himself unable to respond. Instead, he rose from his chair and walked over to the music stand to look at the web page Diane Blacksmith had selected. Until he got there, he was thinking she must have called up an incorrect page. He was wrong. The page was headed 'Oceanic Union Anthem' and was covered in treble and bass staves. Each stave was filled with musical rests. Breve rests were interspersed with quaver and semiquaver rests. Throughout were sprinkled hemidemisemiquaver rests, making the page look as though varying sized black insects were crawling all over it.

At that moment, Tick returned to the room, and requested the group members to stand. When they were all standing to attention, she asked Diane to turn on the music, then proceeded to wave a conductor's baton over the group. Each person solemnly opened and closed their mouths in time. Greg attempted to follow the timing of the baton, but no matter how hard he tried, Tick would admonish him for failing to keep time with the others. Feeling utterly ridiculous, he evidently finally found his rhythm, for eventually Tick stopped complaining at him. Finally, she returned everyone to their seats. "Co-Workers," she said, "I am amazed at your musical integrity. Inspired by our wonderful Department, you have all mastered the OU Anthem already and I declare this Cluster Group ready to proceed to welcome the OU Permits Section delegation next month."

Greg was about to ask when they would be receiving training in OU permit authorisation procedures. But he refrained. "Sometimes," he thought, "I do better to shut up than to put up."

VIII

On the next 8th day, morning sunlight had began streaming though Greg's window at the scheduled time of 8.00 am. He had checked the Enviro-sched which confirmed the sunshine would continue for precisely 9 hours and that the temperature would vary between 19^0 and 23^0. There had been no precipitation scheduled for Suburbia that day.

He completed Nan-ablute and Neighbourhood Physical, then, at his father's suggestion, had lodged an application for a LivUnit. There had been no discussion of the lock out incident. The System had confirmed his application as officially accepted. With nothing further specifically required of him that day, Greg had decided to take his new books to RecSpace. Putting a notebook and pen in his pocket, he had exited the LivUnit. Ignoring the Ubertaxi hovering hopefully outside, he had walked the 3.83 kilometres to the rec area, whistling the new Number 1 from Spotify – **Let's All Pull Together For the Good of The Department.** *He had actually preferred last week's designated Number 1 but couldn't remember it well enough to sing it.*

Though there were few people in sight when he arrived at RecSpace, Greg had known the places would fill rapidly. He had chosen a 3-seater bench right in front of the pond and looked down at the books he held in each hand, wondering which to examine 1st. Knowing 1984 as well as he did, he had opened the Kafka volume, still puzzled by the date in the front. He had turned the pages slowly, looking at the unintelligible text with its strange typeface and unknown letters. Though clearly in a foreign language, words here and there were close enough to English for him to glean some meaning. The title for instance. This book was clearly about some kind of process. 3D printing software code maybe? Nanobuild? Anything was possible, he had supposed.

As he continued to turn the pages curiously, a shadow had passed over him. "Why you reading paperbooks?" said a familiar voice. Greg had looked up to see Trish Abdullah-Goldstein standing in front of him.

"Hello Trish!" he had said with genuine warmth in his voice. "How nice to see you. Aren't you on Litter Patrol?" The girl shook her head. "Don't you read paperbooks?" he asked.

Trish shook her head again. "Nah. Everything's on the i-Comm init?"

"Well this isn't," he had replied, holding out the Kafka volume to her. She had looked at it disdainfully and sniffed. "If it ain't on i-Comm, we don't have to learn it. If I don't hav'ta, I ain't gonna." Greg could see her point.

"How about this?" he had asked, picking up Nineteen Eighty-Four. Trish eyed it suspiciously.

"Is that 1 on i-Comm?" she had asked

"Actually, yes, it is," Greg had replied.

"Why not read it there, then?"

Greg had wondered if all children were as resistant to reading as this. "Well, how about you come sit beside me and I'll read you a bit of it. Then you can see if it sounds better for it to come from a paperbook than from an i-Comm screen."

"How much?"

"How much is what?" Greg had replied.

"How much will you give me to sit next to you?"

Greg had sighed inwardly. This kid should definitely have been born in the days of entrepreneurs. Nonetheless, he felt an urge to help her learn to love reading. "A Thaler?" he had said.

"I usually get 2."

"What do you mean, usually?" he had replied. "I thought you'd never read paperbooks before?"

"I usually get 2 to sit next to someone on a bench in RecSpace."

Greg had known he was being spun a graphene thread. "OK, 2 it is," he had said anyway. "Give me your acc number and I'll make a transfer."

"709-4332-106578/221 – 3," Trish had replied without hesitation.

If you have enjoyed this book, please help others to find it too, by reviewing it at Amazon. At the Amazon web site, simply search on 'Michael Forester', then the name of the book. Even if you have not bought the book on Amazon, you will be able to write a non verified review.

To receive a free copy of Michael Forester's short story collection, Redbuds, visit michaelforester.co.uk and subscribe to the newsletter. Michael Forester will send you a free copy of Redbuds.

Many thanks for your help and time.
Michael Forester

Greg had raised his eyebrows and was glad his MathImplant took the number. "She probably doesn't have an implant yet," he had thought. "She simply knew her account number.' He tapped his screen to make the transfer. It replied with a ping. Trish sat down. Then she looked at him a little oddly and slid right up next to him, her thigh touching his.

"That's a little close, Trish," he had said. The girl had looked disappointed but pulled back to make a 15-centimetre space between them. Greg opened Nineteen Eighty-Four and began reading.

It was a bright cold day in April, and the clocks were striking thirteen. Winston Smith, his shirt collar open in the pleasant warmth of a sunlit day, slipped quickly through the glass doors of Victory Mansions, the nanomats cleansing the soles of his shoes from the swirl of gritty dust that tried to enter along with him.

The hallway was filled with the pleasant smells of roses and honeysuckle wafting from the Olfac. At one end of it a coloured poster, a perfect size for indoor display, had been tacked to the MEN-B. It depicted a smiling face, perfectly proportioned: the face of a man of about forty-five, cleanshaven with ruggedly handsome features. Winston made for the stairs. It was far better for him than using the lift, which saved electricity and the burning of fossil fuel for the benefit of all. It was part of the Pulltogether in preparation for Appreciation Week. The flat was seven flights up. Winston was thirty-nine, was in perfect health having followed the Party 'Healthy Living Ex-Prog' since childhood. Though he knew he could run up the stairs two at a time, he went at a steady pace. There was no benefit to anyone in damaging himself and having to use MedFac unnecessarily. On each landing, opposite the lift-shaft, the poster with the handsome face gazed benignly from the wall. It was one of those pictures which you cannot help being drawn to, feeling safe whenever you saw it. BIG BROTHER IS WATCHING OVER YOU, the caption beneath it ran.

"You ain't reading that." Trish's voice had intruded into his brain. She was right. With his eyes closed, he had been quoting the 1st page of the 1984 he knew by heart and loved so much.

"Sorry, Trish," he had said. "You're absolutely right. This is my favourite book in all the world. I know lots of it by heart. But I promised to read it to you and I will. Let me start again." Greg looked at the text and began again.

It was a bright cold day in April, and the clocks were striking thirteen. Winston Smith, his chin nuzzled into his breast in an effort to escape the vile wind, slipped quickly through the glass doors of Victory Mansions, though not quickly enough to prevent a swirl of gritty dust from entering along with him.

He stopped, frowning. Something wasn't right. Shaking his head a little in confusion, he continued slowly, checking each word carefully.

The hallway smelt of boiled cabbage and old rag mats. At one end of it, a coloured poster, too large for indoor display, had been tacked to the wall. It depicted simply an enormous face, more than a metre wide: the face of a man of about forty-five, with a heavy black moustache and ruggedly handsome features. Winston made for the stairs. It was no use trying the lift. Even at the best of times, it was seldom working, and at present the electric current was cut off during daylight hours.

Greg had stopped again. Someone was playing a trick on him. Someone had written a parody, a travesty of his wonderful, favorite book. "Go on," Trish had said. "I think I might wanna read this."

It was part of the economy drive in preparation for Hate Week. The flat was seven flights up, and Winston, who was thirty-nine and had a varicose ulcer above his right ankle, went slowly, resting several times on the way. On each landing, opposite the lift-shaft, the poster with the enormous face gazed from the wall. It was one of those pictures which are so contrived that the eyes follow you about when you move. BIG BROTHER IS WATCHING YOU, the caption beneath it ran.

Greg had shut the book and looked at Trish. Or rather, he had looked through her as if she wasn't there. Then he got up, picked up the Kafka volume from the bench and walked slowly home, speaking to no one.

As he walked, he had been suddenly conscious of the weight of the books in his hand. He would have been more than sufficiently confused by Der Process alone, a book he could barely understand a few words of. But he was totally floored by the other book. He didn't even want to name it, so devastating a travesty was it of something he had loved so much for so long. Checking various parts of the text again, he had sought specifically for his favourite – the birthday celebration in room 101. He discovered 1st, a reference to the Ministry of Love. He read the familiar words of how the Ministry was responsible for loyalty to Big Brother; how it was a place where there was no darkness. But the words weren't reading right. In this version, there was a sense of cynicism, of fear. "How could there be fear in the Ministry of Love," Greg had wondered. Finally, he had found what he was looking for – the reference to room 101. But this couldn't be right. This wasn't the room where a surprise party was being staged. This was a room in which lay horrible things. "Everyone knows it," he had read. "The thing that is in room 101 is the worst thing in the world."

'No! This can't be right. This isn't what Orwell wrote,' he had thought. "This is appalling. This is anti-Party. This is subversive. This might even be anti-Department."He had been afraid then; afraid to be carrying this vile tract, so far divorced from the true 1984 that he might be held to be non-Compliant; possibly, even a… he could not persuade himself to form the word 'Terrorist.' So preoccupied had he been that it was perhaps not altogether surprising that he had walked straight into a street waste disposal unit and fallen over. The unit had sent an immediate message to the Sanitation Section that it was being vandalised. Before he had time to think of an appropriate course of action, two CommPol officers in full uniform had walked around the corner in front of him.

Greg sighed inwardly. He knew exactly what was coming. He glanced guiltily at his books on the ground beside him, evidence of his non-Compliant status. By the time the CommPol officers reached him, the 1st had unholstered a StunGun, the 2nd an Identilaser. Both immediately pointed their devices at him. The 1st officer looked at him threateningly, saying nothing. He had dropped his head without being asked and the 2nd officer had scanned him. "Co-Worker Gregor Workman 4978-88-915689734. Is this you?" Never had the question felt more superfluous.

"Yes, this is me," Greg had answered.

"Why are you vandalising this Departmentally provided facility?"

"I wasn't," he replied, trying to supress the frustration he was feeling. "I wasn't looking where I was going and I bumped into it."

"Be more careful, Co-Worker," responded the officer. "Are you injured?"

"No, I'm fine," replied Greg. "And yes, I will be more careful. I'm sorry for my error."

"Your error will be logged, Co-Worker. If it is repeated within 1 year of this date, enforcement action will be escalated. HnS regulations require that you now proceed to the nearest HealthFac for medical examination."

Greg had wanted to reply that there was nothing wrong and he just wanted to go home. But he knew better than to argue with CommPol, especially over a Health and Safety issue. "Yes, yes, I will," he had found himself saying. "I'll do that right away." The 2ⁿᵈ officer reholstered his Identilaser. The 1ˢᵗ kept the StunGun trained on Greg as the 2 officers backed away from him. At a distance of precisely 20 metres, the 1ˢᵗ officer had then reholstered the StunGun, and the 2 had turned in unison and marched away.

Greg had stood up, relieved they had not noticed the books. He consulted his i-Comm and changed direction towards the nearest HealthFac. On arrival, the door scanner ran a beam over him. Mercifully, it had not asked vocally for confirmation of his ID, but simply slid to one side, permitting him entry. Greg had stepped out of the sunlight and into a reception area. The door slid closed behind him. Inside, the capacious hall was empty. To his left was a seating area containing 202 seats, all unoccupied. To his right was a pair of swing doors with a notice above them that said 'Clinical Area'. In front was an unstaffed reception desk. He approached and bowed his head, letting the Identiscan pass over him. "Gregor Workman 4978-88-915689734. Is this you?" the mechanical voice had asked.

Greg was growing truly frustrated with the question. But there was no more point in arguing with a machine than there would be with a Compliance Officer. "Yes, this is me," he had answered.

"State the nature of your incapacity," replied the machine.

"I banged my head," replied Greg, feeling a little foolish, and grateful that no one was listening.

"State whether in your opinion you:
1 are unconscious
2 are concussed
3 have cracked your skull
4 are brain damaged
5 are confused
6 are suffering early onset dementia
7 are suffering other symptoms."

Greg had rolled his eyes. He would not have been particularly surprised to hear the machine ask him whether in his opinion he was dead. Again, he had supressed his frustration and answered "Other symptoms."

"State symptoms," responded the machine.

"Slight swelling and mild pain," Greg had replied.

"Do you need to see a medic?" asked the machine.

Greg wondered if the machine could think of any other reason why he might have entered a MedFac on a warm 8th day afternoon when everyone else was outside enjoying the Departmentally supplied sunshine. But all he had said was, "Yes."

"Is your requirement an emergency?" asked the machine.

As soon as he had responded, "No," Greg had regretted it. "Please sit, Co-Worker," said the machine, now sounding irritatingly jovial. "Your estimate waiting time is…" It had hesitated as it calculated. "4 hours 11 minutes and 43 seconds. This facility has been provided to you free of Thaler charge by the Medical Division of the Department."

Greg was waiting for the machine to say "Have a nice day." It didn't. He had sat down in the nearest empty chair, then realised he was sitting in the emergency area. He moved 2 rows back, trying not to wonder why, in an empty MedFac, he was going to have to wait over 4 hours. He passed the time, alternatingly writing in his notebook and grimacing over the pages of this vile bowdlerisation of 1984, whilst every 7.5 minutes, the machine advised him in an irritatingly cheerful voice of the elapsed time and the waiting time that remained.

When the waiting time had fallen to below 1 hour, the update became provided by the minute, preventing him concentrating on anything at all. When there was 1 minute and 43 seconds remaining, he was told to ready himself for attention so as not to waste the valuable time of the Medic who had been allocated to his case by the Department. At 43 seconds, he was advised that the Time Advice Division of the MedFac had provided the updates to him free of Thaler charge. The machine had stated its hope that he had enjoyed his stay in the Facility and expressed a warm wish that it would one day see him again. At 3 seconds, he looked expectantly toward the swing doors that led to the clinical area. At 1.5 seconds, it was pushed open by the most beautiful woman that had ever walked on the earth.

Well, as far as Greg was concerned, she was. Later, when the emotion of the moment had subsided, he had tried to analyse what it was about her that he found so appealing. It wasn't easy. At 175 centimetres, she was of average height. Her body shape followed the traditional female line, and was well within Departmentally approved proportions. But her facial features were not of a distinction that would make her stand out from a crowd. Certainly, her hair was of an approved shade for the week – a yellow blonde called 'Summer'. Though Greg would not have known its official title, he had been aware it was popular for that time of year. Eventually, he had realised there was something in the way she carried herself, an elegance of deportment, that, to his eyes, shone through the formality of the mustard coloured duty tunic and trousers she wore over her regulation heelless flat shoes. She carried a red clipboard which she consulted briefly.

"Gregor Workman 4978-88-915689734?" He had anticipated the question.

"Yes, that is me."

She had frowned. "You have been waiting...4 hours 11 minutes and 43 seconds?"

"Yes, that's right," he had answered.

"Why?"

It was Greg's turn to frown – in confusion. "Err, the machine? It said the waiting time was...?"

"Yes, yes, but why didn't you just tell it you were an emergency? If you don't, it just defaults to the last average waiting time. In this case, yesterday's. I'd happily have seen you as soon as you arrived. There's been no one else here all day."

Greg had sighed inwardly, thinking that there really was no substitute for experience.

"Not to worry. What's the problem?" she had asked. He had explained

the cause of his visit. She took a quick glance at his head there in reception without inviting him into the clinical area. "No bruising... no swelling... no damage to tissue at all. Why did you come here, Co-Worker?"

Greg had closed his eyes and took a deep breath. "The CommPol... HnS..." he started.

She had looked at him with an expression that fell somewhere between sympathy and disdain. "Co-Worker," she had replied, "You really do need to learn that sometimes, the rules are there to be broken."

He had nodded slightly, looking back at her with an expression of his own that fell somewhere between embarrassment and awe.

"Here, take this." She had held her i-Comm out and touched his own with it. "Off you go, now."

With considerable irritation at his singularly unimpressive performance in front of this amazing woman, Greg had risen and made rapidly for the exit. When he glanced back, she had gone. Outside in the sunlight, he had checked his i-Comm to see what meds she had prescribed him. She hadn't. She had given him her i-Comm number.

Greg had all but skipped home in delight. He had never considered himself an attractive man. At 185 centimetres, he could hardly be considered tall. Early signs of premature balding were beginning to thin his black hair at the crown and, though not overweight, it was rather too long since he had regularly followed the Departmental admonition to 'pursue at least one sport at least weekly'. By the time he had arrived at the LivUnit, his new good fortune had entirely pushed from his mind the little bump that had led to it. He had also forgotten, temporarily at least, his preoccupation with the two volumes that had initiated his accident. He wanted nothing more than to i-call the number he had been given immediately. Then he had realised not only that he must look a mess, but also that she (whatever her name might be) might not even be home yet. Reluctantly, he made a particular effort to slow down. Dropping both the books and his clothes on the bed, he stepped into the Nanocleanse and stood thinking, while the invigorating microscopic stream played its warmth down over his head and shoulders, driving the tiredness from his muscles. As he emerged, he had heard his i-Comm bleep with a written message. His 1ˢᵗ thought had been one of abject terror and defeat – she was texting him to tell him not to bother to call. She had had a better offer and would not be available to see him after all. He checked, his heart beating rapidly. It was not. It was from the LivUnit Section of the Department. He had been allocated a studio unit not 2 kilometres from his parents' LivUnit in the direction he had just returned from at the MedFac. He had 24 hours to decide if he wanted to take it.

Greg was feeling high now, higher than he could ever remember feeling before. OK, things were not as stable at work as he might have liked, but his private life was running so well he could have written the script himself. Anticipating the potential of what lay before him, he was just deciding that his happiness could rise no higher when the i-Comm bleeped again. This time, he had recognised the number immediately – it was the one she had given him less than 2 hours ago. Greg deflated immediately. He sat heavily down on the bed holding the i-Comm in both hands. She was texting to tell him she decided not to see him after all. She didn't want him. She was too good for him. He dared not open the message. But then, again, he had dared not not open it. With hands literally shaking, he pressed the message open. It contained a question. In fact, it contained several questions.

"Co-Worker Greg Workman 4978-88-915689734. Is this you? Are you intending to i-Comm me or not? If so, where are you taking me this evening?" It was signed Grete Steele.

Greg had fallen back on the bed, his arms fully extended still holding the i-Comm above him. He let out an involuntary "YES!" then immediately i-Commed her back. "Yes, of course, I am," he wrote. "I'll book a table for 19.00 hours at SocEngage 4. I'll meet you there."

The response was almost instant. "Make it 20.00 hours. And don't forget the permit. We don't want trouble."

It was just as Greg lay back on the bed again, his heart beating faster than he knew it could, that he had heard the music.

61

IX

Greg had returned to the LivUnit that evening to an excited Joe, who demanded a detailed debrief of his day while Grete looked on in undisguised pride. In the days that followed, Greg watched Joe evidently deriving much play area credibility from his father's apparent prominence in the matter of the coming of the Gill-Breathers. Grete, a little less driven by status needs, had simply looked on, clearly enjoying her family's good fortune and happiness. Each night, as Greg returned home, the debrief had continued. Repeating the day's learning had also given Greg an opportunity to assess, with a little perspective, exactly what it was he was being taught.

Lessons in the Oceanic National Anthem had been followed by a single session's tuition in Oceanic systems. From this, Greg had gleaned that Gill-Breathers fell into two groups – Fishpersons and Sharkmen, the latter being equivalent to levs 4-5 in the Departmental Republic. Linguistic tuition in 'Waterspeak' had followed, which Greg eventually understood to be a combination of mouth movements and body inflection. "If you want someone to follow you, for example," he had explained to Joe, "you tap them on the shoulder, open and close your mouth twice, then swim away from them." Joe had been suitably impressed and had rushed off to teach the new language to his classmates at EdFac.

Greg had absorbed it all under the general guise of his newfound personal motto that it was better to shut up than put up. What was more difficult to ignore, however, was the increasingly personal attention that Tick had been paying him. It had been barely noticeable at 1st. A brush of the hand as she passed him something, a seemingly inadvertent touch of the thigh as she sat down, chair number 101 always having been placed next to hers. But the contact had progressed to her hand being placed on his knee and uneasy group hugs at the end of sessions that always seemed to involve longer physical contact with him than anyone else. However, nothing ever seemed to occur that was unequivocal, nothing that amounted to sexual harassment that might have been reportable.

As Month 4 Day 1 drew closer, the Cluster Group had switched its training location to the building's rear staircase just above Waterfloor 1. The members had been instructed to change into Departmentally issued wetsuits.

"It has been decided," explained Tick, "not to issue scuba gear, since this would hinder you in communicating with the OU Delegates and in particular, would impede your singing the Oceanic Anthem in welcome. Instead, from today, we will be developing our ability to hold our breath under water." Training had extended into longer and longer dives down to Waterfloor 1, which Greg found to be surprisingly well lit from the sunlight filtering down through the water. All the old equipment was still in exactly the places it had been left when the waters rose, though now not functioning. Water flora and fauna had become firmly established both inside and outside the building. Greg had been surprised that, with training and practice, he had become able to hold his breath under water for a little over 6 minutes.

A question that remained unanswered in Greg's mind was "What did Gill-Breathers actually look like?" He had long since learned that it was better not to initiate a question in public, but could not help wondering, nevertheless. His mind reverted to Joe's drawing of the fish head with legs.

24 hours before the arrival of the delegation, during the final training session, Greg found himself the only male member of the group, due he was told, to unpredictable absences. Trish issued

final instructions and the group undertook a final dive involving a full rehearsal of the Oceanic Anthem at which the delegation had become adept. After they had finished the training, Tick had delivered her final lecture, encouraging the group to "observe Oceanic procedure" after the welcome formalities were over. Greg went off to the male changing room to shower and dress. He emerged from the shower, drying his hair with a towel that covered his face. When he lowered the towel, it was to see Tick standing in front of him, watching him. She was still in her wetsuit, but the top half was hanging down from her waist, above which she was naked.

Greg stopped, not knowing what to say. A moment's embarrassed silence passed – on Greg's side at least. Then she spoke. "Oh, Co-Worker, do you have a towel I can borrow, please? I've forgotten to bring mine." Greg was glad of an opportunity to break eye contact. He turned away from her, still feeling her eyes on his naked body.

He reached down into his bag and drew out a spare towel. "Here you are, Co-Worker," he managed to say without turning around, reaching his arm out behind him. Tick did not respond. Aching with embarrassment, Greg finally turned to find her standing less than a metre behind him. He jumped back in surprise, banging his head on a clothes hook behind him. Letting out an involuntary "Ow!" he sat down suddenly on the bench. It was exactly the excuse she needed.

"Oh, Co-Worker!" said Trish, a note of alarm in her voice. "Have you hurt yourself? Here, let me look." And with that, she sat down next to him, pulling the towel from him and with it the last vestige of his modesty. Her left hand rose to the back of his head and massaged the spot where she assumed the bump to be, while her right strayed to the front of his torso and began lazily fingering his chest hair.

"Please, don't," he whispered, no longer sure if he meant it or not.

"Ok," she replied, also whispering.

His last lucid thought, or at least the last he could later pinpoint as she withdrew her hands and her head dropped down in front of him, was that her hair shade that week was precisely the same as Grete's.

He must have slept. When he awoke, the light was fading and she was nowhere to be seen. He wanted to convince himself he had imagined it, dreamed it. The problem was, he knew he hadn't. And now he had to catch the last boat and transporter home and somehow explain to Grete what had happened. Greg dressed slowly and deliberately, feeling like a condemned man. He had betrayed his beloved wife. He had wrecked his marriage. She would leave him. She would take Joe away and he'd never see him again. He froze mid thought and repeated it to himself. "If I tell her, she will never let me see my son again. I can't tell her. I'm a liar. I'm a cheat. I have to tell her. But I can't tell her." All the way home, he continued to wrestle with the dilemma. Feeling worse than he could ever remember feeling before and discovering the physical reality of what it meant to have a heavy heart, Greg ascended the steps to the LivUnit and pressed his palm onto the lock. As the door slid, he swallowed hard. This was the moment of decision and he had no idea of what he would do only 10 seconds from now. The door engaged in its recess and he stepped into the Unit.

"Surprise!" they all called out in unison. Suddenly, he was surrounded by smiling faces, some familiar, others unknown. Right in the centre stood his dearest Grete. And standing next to her in an unflattering dingy brown suit, Tick.

Grete walked straight up to him, took him in her arms and kissed him deeply to the cheers of the onlooking crowd. In complete confusion as to what was happening, he let her do so, but did not return the kiss. When she finally released him, she turned to the gathering and said in a loud voice, "Co-Workers, Co-Educators and Co-Educates: Gregor Workman 4978-88-915689734, leader of the Oceanic Delegation to the Department's Permit Section – this is him!" There were more cheers. His right hand was repeatedly shaken, but he didn't really notice by whom. Someone pushed a glass into his left. He did not know what it contained. Everyone wanted to talk to him, congratulate him. Joe danced around him in glee. Grete and several others passed around plates of Authorised Celebration Foodstuffs while the SkypeWAll played stirring music against visuals of happy looking, flag waving young people. Each time Greg looked up to try to catch a word with Grete, she was engaged with someone or something that prevented him. As the group intermingled, Greg found himself standing in front of Tick. She looked him directly in the eye, blinked at him seductively and with no hint of embarrassment asked, "Sleep well, Co-Worker?" Then she smiled knowingly before turning her attention to Joe, who was dancing round, a box over his head with fish heads drawn on it.

In its way, Greg found this no less a threatening a situation than when he was confronted by Neighbourhood Watch for the 1st time. But somehow, this was worse, more sinister. He realised he was suddenly afraid of Tick, what she might be capable of. He began to wonder as to the source of her power, her self-confidence. For the 1st time, he began to question if she might not be more, much more, than she seemed to be.

At 21.00 hours, Grete clapped her hands for attention and said to the group, "Co-Workers, the Departmental Welcome Delegation has an early start tomorrow, so regrettably we must end our festivities earlier than I would have otherwise preferred. Before we do, however, I would like to call on Tick Goldstein to lead the Delegation in a rendition of the Oceanic Union's Anthem. And as the Delegation performs, Co-Workers, please remember you are witnessing one of the 1st professional performances of the Anthem anywhere in the Departmental Republic."

The crowd pulled back to the sides of the room, leaving the members of the Delegation in the centre. Upon the SkypeWAll, there appeared the musical notation of rests for the Anthem. The Delegation members formed up in two rows. Tick tapped her baton twice on an adjacent chair and began conducting. Standing to attention, the Delegation members opened and closed their mouths in unison while the rest of the group looked on in admiring silence. In unadulterated dishonest complicity, Greg kept time with the rest of the group. Finally, Tick put down her baton, turned to the onlookers and bowed to universal extended applause. She turned and gestured towards the Delegation. The applause rose. As it finally subsided, Greg looked round the room. There were few who did not have tears in their eyes.

The following morning, he attended for work, feeling unutterably depressed. Grete had made love to him in her rediscovered proactive manner once again during the night, using up the last of the month's Intimacy Permits. Afterwards, she had again slept undisturbed in his arms such that he felt incapable of interrupting her happiness. On arrival at work, he and the other Delegation Members were escorted by excited Co-Workers to the changing rooms where Tick issued ceremonial wetsuits in the colours of the Departmental Republic. At 10.00 hours, precisely, they dived into the water and swam down to Waterfloor 1. After much training, every member of the group was capable of holding their breath for at least 7 minutes. Greg's personal record was 7 minutes 57 seconds. They swam to the steps of the main entrance to the building, now heavily overgrown with plant life and barnacles, and formed up in their rows. At 10.02, precisely, Greg saw movement ahead of him. Peering through the water, he was able to make out a shoal of what looked like enormous fish. As the shoal approached, he could see it was surrounded by several... several... he was having trouble finding the right word to describe these creatures to himself. From shoulder level upwards, they were indistinguishable from sharks. The torso was human. In the lower body, apparently human legs ending in fins. As the shoal approached, he was increasingly able to make out the composition of the bodies of the individual creatures. Again, the upper part of the bodies and heads were fish-like. Similar to the shark creatures, the legs also ended in fins that they used to propel themselves. Greg had no time to decide if he was fascinated or repulsed. As the shoal approached, Tick motioned the Delegation to attention and began wielding her baton in water-constrained slow motion while the Delegation members opened and closed their mouths in unison. The shoal swam past them without acknowledging them and on into the building. The only indication that their existence had been noticed came from the Sharkmen (at least, Greg presumed that was what they were) who each turned to check them with apparent suspicion as they passed. It was all over in less than 30 seconds. 4.00 minutes had elapsed since they dived. Tick ushered the group back into the building and directed them to swim up to the surface. She waited on the landing of floor 2, for them all to emerge from the water then said, "And there you have it, Co-Delegates. You are the 1st to welcome our esteemed Oceanic Co-Workers to the Departmental Republic, now merged by democratic assent with the Oceanic Union. I am honoured to be authorised to tell you on behalf of the Department, that the Departmental Republic is, as of today, dissolved. We are now the 1st Departmental State, Oceanic Union, for which the authorised shortened reference is 1stDep. And you, esteemed Co-Workers, are now Co-Workers of the Oceanic Union. All over the City at this moment, announcements like this are being made. Spontaneous celebrations will be breaking out everywhere. All i-Comms, all SkypeWAlls, will carry the same DepCasts." Trish threw her arms wide open and declared in a warm empathic voice, "Co-Workers, the Oceanic Union welcomes you all!"

By now, though her face was still wet, it was evident Trish had tears streaming down from her eyes. Around Greg, the members of the Delegation were shaking hands. From behind him, the doors to the Travel Permit Section swung back and Co-Workers pushed through cheering, everyone trying to get to the Delegation to shake their hands. Outside, a flotilla of small boats carried military bands, jazz bands, string quartets and full orchestras. Every musician had i-Comms in front of them turned to the page for the music of the Silent Oceanic Anthem and every instrument was silent. But inside the building, music had been turned on. All around Greg, people were dancing, singing, celebrating the historic merger.

Greg had never felt more isolated in his life.

X

He had frozen in the moment, as motionless as when he had last heard the tune. It was drawing closer now. In desperation, he had hoped the music was not for him: the slow, ponderous melody that seemed to sway back and forth, as if summoning out dancers everywhere. Despite his desperation, he had known the music was for him. Louder and louder. He had not known why. Closer. It had come closer. He must have done something non-Compliant. Then, the rumbling of the heavy vehicle had shaken the street. He must be a criminal. The smell of fossil fuel mingled with exhaust fumes had drifted in through the open window. But he wasn't a criminal. The vehicle had stopped. He didn't know what he had done. He didn't know what he had done. Doorbell; voices in the shared room; his father calling, calling his name; then, another voice; harsher; deeper. Louder. He didn't know what he had done.

"Gregor Workman, 4978- 88-915689734. Is this you?"

His response had been too slow. Something heavy had hit the partition door. Then, again.

"Greg Workman, 4978- 88-915689734. This is you." The voice was cold, metallic. "If you have any weapons, put them down now. If you are holding your satchel, put it down, now. If you are holding anything else, put it down, now. Stand away from the door. Face away from the door. Do not approach the door. Raise your arms to 45° below horizontal. Spread you fingers apart, palms facing behind you. Open your mouth wide. If you attempt to use a weapon, you will be Retired without further warning."

He had heard the sound of the partition door being slid back and felt the movement of air as a presence had entered, silent upon the carpeted floor. Then, something pointed pushed into the small of his back.

"Do not speak." Gloved hands, rough expert hands, hands that knew

70

precisely what they were seeking, slid intrusively over his body from the crown of his head downwards. Fingers splayed over his face, pressing the side of his nose, his ears. A finger was inserted roughly into his right ear; then the left; then each nostril. Two fingers intruded into his open mouth causing him an intense vomiting reflex response. He resisted the urge to throw up, terrified of the consequences of losing control. Arms surrounding him from behind. Palms slid simultaneously over his nipples as the fingers explored his chest, then found the join in his shirt and pulled hard. Buttons flew forward over the floor, over the bed. His shirt was tugged roughly backwards over his splayed arms. The hands had continued their slow, demeaning journey downwards. The fingers entered his belt buckle. Hands at each side of him pulled down hard on his trousers, drawing them down to the floor. Thumbs inserted into the waistband of his underpants pulled them down, too to where they rested on top of the bunched trousers at his feet.

"Bend forward to 90°." He had Complied instantly. His field of vision had slid down over his bed to the floor. The fingers, playing like insects over his waist, hips. His buttocks had been parted. The expert finger had pushed roughly into his anus; pain; withdrawn; more pain. The fingers felt around his scrotum, a palm lifting his testicles as if weighing them, massaging them. Then, the palms had slid down his right leg; left leg.

"Stand straight. Lift right leg. Point the sole of your foot backwards. Balance with your hands on the bed if you need to." Fingers had splayed his toes, slid in between each one; pain. "Now the left leg." Splayed toes; more pain. "Stand up, straight. Do not turn around. Do not reposition. Do not reach for any weapons. If you reach for your weapon you will be Retired without warning." A sound like tapping; an electronic pen hitting the surface of a screen. The gloved hands had reached round him and placed an i-Comm onto the bed. "Identiprint this. You will receive a copy."

Cold silence lapped like a shallow lake round his knees. Cold; his feet had felt cold; then, a bleep from his i-Comm; a second.

The 1ˢᵗ, an officially headed Departmental Memo.

'I hereby confirm that on a routine visit to LivUnit 88-915689734 my person and premises were courteously and respectfully inspected by representatives of the Neighbourhood Watch and that I willingly relinquished items requested for further examination. I was informed and understood clearly that these items will be examined, and may or may not be returned to me and may or may not be presented in evidence in my forthcoming trial.'

At the bottom of the i-Comm was his own identiprint.

The second was a message from Grete. 'It's 20.30, you monstrous insect. Why in JeKAllah's name have you stood me up?'

He had risen from the bed, unconscious of the fact that he was still naked until he had walked into the shared room. His parents were standing in the centre of the room, holding each other in silence, also naked, their clothes in two heaps around their feet. His mother had slowly raised her head from his father's shoulder and looked into his eyes for several moments. Then she had screamed. She had screamed for a long, long time.

XI

That evening, Greg had not needed his family to tell him he was on the DepCasts. The Transporter Comm links on the Trams were carrying virtually nothing but the celebrations. Inevitably, on his arrival at LivUnit, Joe had 1st danced around him in circles, then grabbed his hand and dragged him to the sofa to cross-question him on every possible aspect of his experience that day. He was particularly interested in the Sharkmen, asking for a detailed description of their appearance and whether Greg had seen them eat anyone. Greg found himself wondering if they ever did.

As the days rolled forward and his celebrity status led to requests for appearances and interviews, the right opportunity to talk honestly with Grete never seemed to arrive. With a guilty heart, he allowed the truth of his betrayal to slouch shamefully into the back of his mind, until the memory seemed, somehow, less confrontational. At work, further meetings of the cluster group had been called, as they moved on to the more practical phase of their responsibilities – the observation of Oceanic procedure and dissemination of the learning to their Co-Workers. To Greg's relief, Tick had neither mentioned their previous encounter nor attempted further intimacy with him. She had simply treated him like any other member of the group as she issued detailed instruction on what they were to do during the observation exercises. All the instruction seemed to amount to no more than simply to observe and report, 1st, to the cluster group itself, then to groups of Co-Workers throughout the Travel Permits Section.

The next morning at 10.00 hours, they dived once more to Waterfloor 1 and watched the Sharkmen usher the shoal of

Fishpersons into the building. Since several days had elapsed, Greg was expecting to find that the Gill-Breathers had rearranged the floor and imported their own equipment. It was not so. As they swam into what had been Travel Permit Section floor 1, he was surprised how good the visibility was. By some method that was not immediately obvious, sunlight was being refracted through the windows, most of which remained intact. Greg's 1st impression was of there being no change to the organisation of the floor. Desks, workstations, partitions, all stood undisturbed, so far as he could tell, in their original positions. His 2nd impression came from the level of activity, the sense of busyness all around him from the unending movement of the Fishpersons. In each direction he looked, numerous of the half fish, half human creatures were engaged in swimming from one end of the floor and back again under the watchful observation of Sharkmen posted strategically around the large room. Others were occupied picking up and putting down i-Comms from which no sound emerged and opening and closing their mouths voicelessly into them. Still more were studying screens carefully, screens that were entirely blank. More Fishpersons endlessly opened and closed cupboards and cabinets, neither extracting nor depositing anything as they did so. And all, periodically, swam up to the Sharkmen, made the sign for 'no change' and then returned to their work. After several minutes of observation, Greg and his companions returned to the surface for air, then immediately dived again.

This time when they arrived, the floor was deserted. Tick motioned the group down into the building's basement canteen where all the Fishpersons had assembled, once again under the close observation of the Sharkmen, who had positioned themselves at the exits. In the canteen, the Fishpersons were seated at the tables. Some were eating water plants. All were looking at one another, earnestly opening and closing their mouths. No sound emerged and Greg saw nothing that suggested the conveyance of meaning. At the end of the canteen, a Sharkman struck a large gong, sending vibrations through the water. In unison, the Fishpersons rose and swam out of the door and up the stairs, while the Sharkmen continued to bar every potential exit. The Cluster Group followed them back to Waterfloor 1 where each Fishperson re-engaged in their previous activity. Tick motioned to the group to follow her back to the surface. As Greg swam out of the doors and up the stairs, he was more conscious than ever of the complete silence of the watery environment he was being asked to study.

"Shower and change please," instructed Tick as they emerged from the water, "and assemble on floor 3 as normal." Greg glanced around himself uneasily, checking for reassurance that the other male members in the group were still present. All 3 were still there. Feeling cautious but relatively safe, he entered the male changing rooms, showered and dressed. He then made his way to the Cluster Group room where Tick was already present. When the group had reassembled, she asked, "Right. What did you observe?" Greg could have made many remarks at that moment. Few of them particularly polite.

"Astonishing," said a woman to his right.

"Quite remarkable," echoed the man next to her.

"I concur," said Greg ambiguously, trying to keep his voice sounding neutral.

"I've never seen such activity," said the young woman sitting on his right.

"If we could learn to work like that," said an older non-bi next to the right, "our productivity would rise almost immeasurably."

"Aye," acknowledged several other group members simultaneously.

Greg studied each as they spoke. They were all entirely serious. He looked at each face around the room in turn. Everyone appeared to be absolutely genuine in their enthusiasm for Gill-Breather procedures.

"I'm delighted you learned so much so quickly," said Tick. "Our job now is to record and disseminate the working methods of the Gill-Breathers amongst our colleagues, so that we can all learn to work as efficiently as they do. And Co-Workers, no one is expecting this to happen instantly. This is going to be challenging. The Department understands it will take time for us to learn to perform at the standard of the Gill-Breathers. The Department acknowledges that, after all, we are only human. If anyone would like further explanation or to discuss these issues further, you will find me in my office on Floor 4 room 101." This last she said looking directly at Greg.

For his part, Greg simply followed the other Cluster Group members out of the large room and down the stairs to floor 2, where his colleagues awaited his debrief.

XII

Greg had picked up his parents' undergarments and handed the clothing to them wordlessly. At that moment, he could think of nothing soothing to say. They had seemed to him suddenly to have aged more than he could conceive. There had been an air of helplessness about them, an unthinking conformity to the way in which they followed his direction to dress. When they were once again clothed, he had sat them in front of the SkypeWAll and Googled Protector of the Republic. Then, he had left them watching while he explored the Nutriprep area for anything he could give them that might help them to recover. At the back of a cupboard, his hand had alighted on a box of teabags that could have been of just about any age at all. Greg made his parents mugs of hot tea with far more than the recommended amount of sugar, then wondered what to do next. His mother was weeping quietly in front of the SkypeWAll, his father sitting straight backed next to her, saying nothing. Neither appeared to be watching the programme. He had concluded his continued presence would only serve to remind his mother of the ordeal she had just experienced. But he could not risk exiting the LivUnit during Curfew, particularly not so soon after a visit from Neighbourhood Watch. Reluctantly, he returned to his room, the site of his own violation, and tidied up the mess that the 'courteous and respectful' inspection had left him with. As he returned his books and papers to their correct places on the shelf he noticed 1st, the absence of several notebooks – those he had already filled with his observations. Then, he realised that both Nineteen Eighty-Four and Der Process were missing.

Greg had returned the mattress to his bed from the corner of the room where it had been slashed open and dumped, replaced the torn bedding and sat on it, his elbows on his knees, his head in his hands. What had he done to merit such treatment? He was a loyal Co-Worker of the Departmental

Republic. All he wanted to do was serve the Department and his fellow citizens well. Why was he being treated like a Subversive, a Terrorist even? Not that he had ever actually met anyone from either category. He lay back, facing the ceiling. "Suppose," he thought. Then stopped himself. No. It wasn't possible. Not in a place like the Departmental Republic. The Department loved its citizens. It wanted the very best for them. But the thought persisted, tapping on the window of his consciousness until he granted it entry.

"Suppose there were a Republic." He had thought. "Not the Departmental Republic of course. But just suppose for a moment, that a different Republic wanted to keep its citizens on message, Compliant; to remind everyone – for the good of everyone of course – that non-Compliance cannot be tolerated. But then, what if that Republic – not the Departmental Republic, of course – had not always been there. Then, suppose that before this hypothetical Republic had been established, people thought differently. Suppose they were ignorant of the value of the order that Compliance brought. Then, just possibly, much of what had been written before the Departmental era brought Enlightenment and wisdom to all could have been contrary to Departmental doctrine. It would be ignorant. Primitive. Untrue. You could burn it of course, or try to suppress it. But there might still be diehards who would resist; who would cling on to their ignorant beliefs. Maybe, you'd do better to re-write it, so that it was Compliant. Compliant people would take little convincing that the texts had originally been written in the new way, or more likely would not care. Diehards would take longer. But they would die out eventually. And in time, all copies of the original texts would get lost, or be destroyed. All for the good of Co-Workers of course."

"Perhaps, that was it," he had slowly permitted himself to consider. Perhaps, some books – just a few books of course – adopted a dangerous, non-Compliant viewpoint. 'Perhaps,' Greg had thought, "that's why, there are Subversives and Terrorists in the world. "Perhaps," they have simply been misled, taught ignorance from non-Compliant books. Perhaps I have simply been unfortunate enough to stumble upon some of these non-Compliant books."

78

However, it made him see George Orwell in a completely different light, if he truly had written the original Nineteen Eighty-Four about a totalitarian society that supressed its citizens mercilessly. And the society that Orwell described, well, anyone would want to criticise it, wouldn't they? In a context of poverty, it imposed its merciless will upon the majority, controlling every action and thought for the benefit of a tiny minority of Inner Party members. Why, it even forced its more intelligent citizens to collude in a façade of open dishonesty, whilst never being able to admit the truth that was obvious to all. It made him profoundly glad that he lived in an age of tolerance, freedom of thought and an indulgent Department that took away so many worries from its Co-Workers. But he could hold the thought only momentarily. Fleeting gladness collided instantly with his recollection of the 1ˢᵗ Retirement he had seen in the PlayFac with his father; his own encounter with Neighbourhood Watch; the abusive intolerant strip search his whole family had just had to endure. He might have been able to continue believing if it had been he alone who had suffered such an indignity. But to induce such terror in the hearts of such Department-loving, Compliant Co-Workers as his parents, that was… unforgivable. Eventually, the whole edifice had come crashing down, floor by floor, as the foundations of his faith in everything familiar finally crumbled. For if the Department could act in a way that was unforgivable, it meant the Department was not always right. It was fallible. And if it was not always right, in what other matters than this might it be it wrong? As uncertainty drove an iron wedge further and further under the open door of his doubt, his conscious mind had begun to scrabble around on the floor of his memory, looking for that which was dirty, sordid; that which was non-Compliant, but yet consistent with his new realisations. His search did not go unrewarded.

Greg scanned mentally though his life experience – a 1ˢᵗ degree in Modern Departmental History followed by a Masters in Observational Systems, and a PhD in the Comparative Procedural Systems of groups 1 and 4 of the Permits Section; a Departmentally owned and provided home with 2 parents of exemplary Compliance; a Departmentally monitored Internet that told him monthly, daily, hourly, by the minute what everyone else was doing in dress style, in entertainment, in nutrition. The pressure to Comply was subtle but intense; the pressure to match the behaviour, beliefs and thinking of one's peers. He had stopped, realising he finally had the issue by the scruff of its neck. Everything in his life, everything around him, everything he had ever known was focussed on encouraging him to Comply. And clearly, for most people, it worked. For most people felt, unconsciously, a profound need to belong to the group, to be approved of by peers, to be the same as others around them. "But what," thought Greg, "of the few that do not? What can the Department do with them... with me? Am I the 1st, the only person in Departmental history who derives no satisfaction, no sense of identity from conformity? Truth is," he had thought, "I'm just different. I don't match up. I am ... I am a mis-matcher." Mismatcher. Mismatcher. Had he coined a new word? He i-Commed quickly to the Universal Dictionary of DepSpeak. The word did not exist. A dark thought clouded his mind, a lump formed that reached from his solar plexus up to his throat. Perhaps the on-line Dictionary was even at that instant messaging Neighbourhood Watch of his search for a non-existent, and non-Compliant word. Surely, this was true evidence that he was indeed a Subversive, perhaps well on his way to becoming a Terrorist.

Over and over his mind had turned through the night. So, what if he was right? Non-conformity wasn't everything. Could he, a mismatcher, not learn to live with Compliance for the sake of an easy life, a comfortable life in a society where everyone else disagreed with him? Surely his time would pass more easily, more enjoyably if he simply conformed to Departmentally inspired norms. Surely the Department was right, anyway; maybe not about everything but about, well, most things. Independent thinking wasn't everything. Truth wasn't everything. Honesty wasn't every-. He stopped, disgusted by his own obsequiousness. Someone, something was illuminating the dark dungeon of his mind that he had not even realised was a dungeon. Someone was granting him a new vision, a new understanding of the truth and he was about to throw it back in whatever face that nameless entity had, for the sake of… of… comfort? He couldn't believe his own moral paucity. That woman, Grete, had been right and she'd met him only once. She knew he was just a monstrous insect that even JeKAllah, if he/she/they existed, couldn't forgive. His social currency was exhausted. He was a moral Vagrant. He might as well go out into Curfew and walk the streets until Neighbourhood Wat- . His stream of self-loathing was dammed instantly by the bleep of a text. He looked down. It carried Grete's ID.

His finger hovered over the button as he wondered what the consequences might be of opening the i-Comm message. Curiosity overcame him.

'I'm sorry,' it said. 'I was angry and rude and that's unforgivable. There must have been a perfectly good reason why you didn't come. I want to give you a chance to explain. I really want to get to know you properly. Please answer this.'

Greg 1st felt relief, and then dread as he thought about how he might explain the evening's events and the reason for his nonattendance at SocEngage 4. He checked the time – it was 03.03. Taking a deep breath, he messaged back, 'I'm so sorry. My home was raided by Neighbourhood Watch for no good reason. I and my parents were strip searched and our LivUnit ransacked.' He read it over, finding it difficult to believe himself. He deleted the second sentence and wrote, 'I and my parents were abused. I was preoccupied with mum and dad's distress afterwards and unable to let you know at the time. I can't apologise enough for letting you down.' He read it through again. It wasn't much more credible but at least it explained his behaviour. Grete would either believe it or not. That was her decision alone. He instructed the i-Comm to send the message and sat with the device in his hands, awaiting a response. He watched, counting the seconds until a minute had passed, then a 2nd. As the end of the 3rd minute approached, he was reluctantly concluding that she was not going to respond, when the device bleeped him a notification of receipt of message. It listed her ID. The relief and dread both returned as without delaying, he pressed 'open'.

'I've never heard anything in my life that sounded so preposterous. It's so outrageous a slander of our protectors, the Neighbourhood Watch, that

I can't believe you would try to lie to me about it. So, for now, I'm going to believe you. Meet me at SocEngage 4 for breakfast at 07.00 hours. 1ˢᵗ light is 06.42, so you'll not need Curfew permit, and the SocEngage Permit is good for 24.00 hours from last night. I don't expect you've slept much, so I'll leave you to decide whether it's more important to sleep or to meet me. Let me know which, so I don't waste my time again. And if you do decide to come, I'm going to want to hear the whole story of how you've got yourself into this mess. The only response you are permitted to make to this message is either 'Yes,' or 'No'.

Greg returned the one word response immediately and settled down in his bed. Just as he was about to fall asleep, he sat bolt upright. Then he set his alarm for 06.15.

The alarm shook him awake at the anticipated time. He threw back the bedding and rolled onto the floor to make sure he didn't allow himself to fall asleep again. Then he leapt straight into the Nanocleanse for a pre-set 30 second cleansing. Dressing silently, he listened at the door of his parents' partition until the sound of deep breathing reassured him that they were at least managing to sleep after their evening's ordeal. At precisely 06.42, he opened the door of the LivUnit to find the ground carpeted in white as far as he could see. He groaned in frustration that he had forgotten to check the weather prediction for the day as he looked down at his light clothing and footwear. There was no time to change clothes, now. He simply exchanged his shoes for boots, then stepped out into 4.7 centimetres of snow. As he trudged off in the direction of the Suburbia Plaza, on his i-Comm he summoned the 1ˢᵗ Ubertaxi he saw. It ignored him, being pre-booked. He issued a general summons for any Ubertaxi in the vicinity. The 2ⁿᵈ. and the 3ʳᵈ both ignored him. Finally, the system seemed to take pity on him as a taxi hovered its way smoothly round the corner, oblivious to the snow. As it neared, he saw it was a night taxi still out looking for premium fares or 'Undereducates like me', he berated himself. On reaching him, the vehicle paused and hovered while he climbed in. "SocEngage 4," he instructed. Its light changed from green to red and it floated off silently in the direction of the AmaBay Mall, dropping him right outside the door at 06.58. He sped through the doors and straight to the lifts where he instructed 'SocEngage 4, floor 8', as if the machine did not know its location. He counted the seconds as the lift rose silently to the 8th floor, stepping out of the doors at 06.59.37. Grete was sitting, dressed for work, cross-legged at a table 2 rows back from the lift and saw him instantly. As he approached, she smiled at him in a guarded fashion, then checked the time on her i-Comm. "Soya latte, please," she said.

"And after all that," he finished, "I still have no idea why they are persecuting me nor what I am charged with."

She had been virtually silent for a long time. 1st, she had requested, in polite tones, an explanation of his absence the evening before. Then, he had simply found himself needing to go back to earlier and earlier events to provide some sort of context to the previous evening's outrage. Eventually, he had ended up telling her the story of his life. All the while, she had sat silent and attentive, sipping occasionally on her coffee. Now he too fell silent, looking at her with the attention he had been unable to pay her while he concentrated on what he was saying. As her spell began to fall on him once again, he became increasingly aware of something unusual, something unknown happening in a deep place inside, an event and a place for which he had no prior experience and therefore, no name. Later, still unable to put a precise term on it, all he would be able to tell himself was that it felt like, without knowing anything about her, he had known her all his life. Without knowing if she was trustworthy, he was willing to trust her with his most precious secrets. Without knowing if she would or could reciprocate, he wanted to share everything he had, everything he was with her.

"I see the dilemma." He shook himself back into the real time of the coffee date as she spoke. "Something in all this is untrue." He held his breath, thinking she was going to say she did not believe him. "You're trying to hold onto everything you believe, everything you have been taught about the Department. Yet, if it is true, that means you yourself are at fault in a

major way – like you're a Vagrant, or a Subversive or maybe even a Terrorist. But you have no intention to be so and you can't see how anyone else can think you so. So, you're left having to believe either you are at fault and you don't know why, or the Department – in this case, the Permits Section and Neighbourhood Watch – are at fault in pursuing you."

"Yes," he said with relief that she wasn't accusing him of dishonesty. "You have it exactly right."

"So," she answered, "which is easier to believe? You being at fault or the Department?"

"Well, me of course," he responded.

"Fine. You're a Subversive and I'm off to work. Have a nice life – though I expect it will be a short one." She was not smiling but nor did she move. She finished the last of her latte. His flat white lay untouched on the table in front of him. "So, now tell me what you really think."

"She has me," he thought. "She can see exactly what I'm thinking. It's impossible to lie to this woman." He looked at her directly. "I think, Grete, that Neighbourhood Watch has made a mistake."

"And that opinion, Greg," she replied, "should be enough to make me get up and leave immediately. But let's say that for now, you have my attention. Such a 'mistake,' which we both know is impossible anyway, does not explain why both the reason for, and outcome of your disciplinary process at work were redacted."

"The Permits Section has also made a mistake," he replied.

"And that, my dear," she said, as she rose from the table, "makes you a Subversive with whom I must not associate."

He collapsed inside. Somebody wonderful was about to walk out of his life and he had barely had a chance to get to know her. He wanted to say so much: to dissuade her from leaving, to tell her he understood, to express his regret. But all he could manage was, "And will I see you again?"

"Oh, yes, of course," she answered with a smile. "You still owe me dinner. 20.00 hours tonight at SocEngage 1. You make the reservation and get the permits. And oh, yes. You're paying."

He had made the booking from work, wincing at the menu prices. "Well, it is SocEngage 1," he reasoned with himself. "And she's worth it." The evening's conversation had focussed as much on her as the morning's had on him. She seemed to sparkle in front of him when she smiled, driving his worries from his mind, at least temporarily. He had pointed out to her the coincidence of their names, but she had never read Metamorphosis Reversed. In fun, he asked her if she had the medical skills to transform him from being a monstrous insect into a human being and if so, would she please marry him quickly. She didn't laugh. Instead, she looked at him without blinking and asked if that was a proposal of marriage. He had turned red and fumbled for an answer that never came. Then it was her turn to laugh. But it had been easy, comfortable laughter that ended with him holding her hand across the table; a hand that he did not let go of until it was time to leave. When he had authorised a larger Thaler deduction from his account than he had expected, the SocEngage waitbot ordered them a taxi and asked for the destination address. Before he could speak, she had leant across him and given her own. On arrival at her LivUnit, she had invited him in for coffee. Greg had acknowledged silently to himself that it would have been impolite of her not to and that nothing more was implied than coffee. He had accepted. It would have been impolite of him not to when nothing more was implied than coffee. And she did indeed offer him coffee – a choice of either Java medium or Sumatran full heavy. He had asked her to decide. Then they had both leaned back on her large sofa, talking like old friends. Finally, reluctantly, he acknowledged it was time for him to leave. He had risen and put his coat on, then walked to the door. She had followed silently in stockinged feet, so that when he reached the door, he did not know she was immediately behind him. As he turned to bid her goodnight, he found her standing just centimetres in front of him, looking up directly into his face. "What time is your Curfew Pass good until?" she had asked.

Until that moment, his preoccupation with her and the evening had driven the thought of Curfew from his mind. "00.00 hours," he had answered.

"Shame it's 10 after, then," she said as she reached behind him to lock the door.

They had slept little but nevertheless, had woken before the dawn. When he had made love to her again, she had asked, "What will you do now?"

"Well, if I can use your Nanocleanse, I'll go directly to work from here," he had answered.

"No, I mean about the other. Your problem. Your trial."

Her question had made him realise he had been avoiding the issue, stealing a little happiness from the gods of fear for as long as he could make himself forget. But he had known that with the dawn, he would once again have to pay due fealty to those gods.

He thought before answering. "They say I will be put on trial, but they have not said what for or when. They have taken books from me that I think they intend to use at the trial, but I don't know how. They must surely intend to present evidence and maybe even produce witnesses that support their contention that I am guilty. But I do not know what that evidence is, or what any witnesses might testify to. I cannot prepare a defence beyond telling my personal story as I did to you last evening and expressing my loyalty to the Department as vehemently as possible. But Grete, I have no confidence that it will achieve anything. I don't think anyone's going to be listening. It feels like the script of my life has already been written... like... like I'm living inside the pages of a book."

She looked at him with what seemed admiration, perhaps, for the lucidity of his speech. "Well, talk to them like that at your trial and they'll have to listen," she said. "And in the meantime, do the only things you can do."

"Which are?"

"Work diligently. Live Compliantly. Make love to me." And with that she pulled him down on top of her.

For the 1st time he could remember, he was late for work.

Returning home that evening, Greg found his parents much as he had left them, with the same air of geriatric confusion about them that he had 1st seen when he had come upon them naked in the main room of the LivUnit the previous evening. He had made a light supper for them and supervised their withdrawal to their Partition. Their condition worried him deeply. Then, he realised he had all but forgotten about the offer of a LivUnit of his own. He reached for his i-Comm and called up the Accommodation Department's page. He was all but ready to hit the 'Accept' button when a message flashed onto the screen in front of him: 'Offer Withdrawn'. Instantly, Greg was filed with rage at the injustice of his treatment. His 24 hours option time had not elapsed. This was intervention in due Departmental Process. It wasn't supposed to happen. Someone was wielding influence to his detriment. "Everyone's equal under the law. Everyone's innocent until proven guilty," he said out loud with extreme irritation in his voice. Then, he wondered, for the 1st time whether his trial might already have taken place, for how would he know; whether he had already been found guilty – of JeKAllah-knows-what, but guilty nonetheless. And perhaps they were simply going through administrative preparations for his arrest and incarceration. What other explanation could there be for the withdrawal of the offer? He threw his i-Comm down on the bed in disgust and stamped into the main room where he threw the sofa cushions onto the floor and stamped his feet some more until two things happened. The 1st was that a voice in his head told him he was behaving like a 2.5-year-old. The 2nd was that he noticed an icy draught. It was coming from the front door. The door was open. In his anger, he cursed himself for not locking it when he had come in earlier. But when he reached it, he glanced towards his parents' partition. The door there was open too. He felt as icy inside as the draught did outside. Then he ran to his parents' Partition. Whilst the bed had earlier been lain in, it was unoccupied. His parents were gone.

"What can they be thinking of?" was his 1st reaction, until he remembered their mental state and realised they probably weren't thinking of anything at all. It was only then he checked their room to find to his shock, his total and absolute terror, that their satchels and tablets were gone,

too. Immediately, he called Neighbourhood Watch. Then he sat with his head in his hands and wept.

2 hours later, a Neighbourhood Watch vehicle, a less aggressive version than those of his previous encounters, stood with its blue lights flashing and its engine running outside the LivUnit, the fumes of its exhaust no less noxious than those of the Watch's more confrontational units. At Greg's call for help, Grete had come immediately on Emergency Curfew Pass. A female Officer of the Watch brought Greg and Grete mugs of tea – their 3rd since the officers had arrived. As she handed the mugs to them, a male officer walked into the LivUnit without knocking. His eyes met those of his female colleague and he shook his head slightly. He entered the Unit and sat on an upright chair opposite Greg and Grete on the sofa.

"Greg Workman," he started, his tone softer than Greg could ever recall from any Neighbourhood Watch or CommPol Officer he had encountered before, "4978- 88-915689734, Is this you?"

Greg looked up, fighting back the tears in his eyes. "That is me," he managed to answer, choking on his words.

"It is my duty to inform you that we have found your parents, Alfred Jonas Workman, 1084- 88-915689734 and Sophia Jayne Workman, 1263-88-915689734, seated on a bench in RecArea 2. Both their satchels were open. Both their tablets had been taken." The Watch Officer hesitated to allow for a response. Neither Greg not Grete made any. "They were both Retired before we arrived. The Medic pronounced life extinguished at 23.22.04. I am genuinely sorry."

Greg looked up but did not speak.

"Is there anyone you would like me to call?"

After a moment, he shook his head.

"Do you wish an Officer of the Watch to remain with you?"

He shook a second time.

The female officer laid her hand gently on his, then both the officers withdrew.

After a while, when all was silent, Grete locked the door. Then she took him by the hand and led him to his parents' Partition and lay down with him on the bed, holding him, as he sobbed until dawn washed the darkness away.

As first light rose, Greg had finally stopped weeping and was asleep. Grete had extricated herself from his arms, whereupon, in his sleep, he had gripped the bedclothes in tight fists like an unsettled child. By the time he emerged from the sleep Partition, his face still tear stained, she had already sent an i-Comm to the Permit Section to advise he was in no state to attend work. She then tidied away the remaining signs left from the prior evening's traumas. If he had had thoughts for anyone but himself at that moment, Greg might have wondered if Grete was reconsidering the wisdom of allowing herself to become embroiled in the complexity and confusion of his life. But he did not. He was too numb for thought. She passed him a mug of tea and sat with him in silence while he drank it, too inwardly focussed to realise just how far she was drawing on her trauma training to manage his behaviour. Eventually, when he had finished his drink, she took him back to the sleeping Partition, where he stood passively while she removed his clothes and ushered him gently into the Nanocleanse, letting the particle flow work its way into his tense muscles. Then she threw his clothes, together with her own, into the launderer and followed him into the Nanocleanse. As they emerged he spoke for the 1st time that morning. "Will you marry me?" he asked.

She answered without hesitation. "Yes, but not yet," then laid out clothes on the bed for him to dress himself, as she proceeded to remove hers from the launderer, folded and ironed. When they were both dressed, she asked, "What do you want to do today? Do you want to go out?" He nodded. "A walk? Taxi? Where do you want to go?"

"Walk," he replied. "We're not going far."

It was less than 1.74 kilometres to RecArea2, but it took them 44 minutes and 27 seconds to reach it, Greg stopping every few paces to take deep gulps of air, as a drowning man surfacing periodically might do. Grete's arm was linked thorough his and she was supporting him as he walked. There was little of note to catch the eye when they arrived. RecArea2 consisted of a sparsely grassed zone for the exercise of pets which contained trees and faeces disposal bins. Further in was a small lake, behind which was a copse, too thick with brambles to walk into. In front of the lake were benches. Around the perimeter of it all ran a shoulder-high fence. "How did they get in when it was locked for Curfew?" Grete wondered aloud. Greg nodded to a breach in the fence, 1.1 metres high. "They crawled?" He did not answer, but instead strode forward to the lake, making directly for the 2nd bench where he stood with his hands on the backrest. "Why here?" she risked asking, as she joined him.

He was silent a moment. "47 years, 2 months and 11 days," he replied.

She put her hand on his and looked into his eyes. "I don't understand," she said softly. "Please tell me – if you want to."

"They dated their marriage from the day she proposed to him. Here. It was called a 'park' back then. I've heard the story more times than I can remember. She went down on one knee and proffered him a single rose. He accepted on the spot. They walked home to his LivUnit – although they were called houses then, and they never spent a night apart again. Not even last night."

"And that was…"

"47 years, 2 months and 11 days ago," he finished for her. Then he pushed the bench forward. It came away easily from its footings and rolled down the slight incline, falling into the lake, where it disappeared below the surface. "Why are they doing this?" he asked without looking at her as the last ripples lapped against the shoreline. "Me – they think I'm a Subversive. I can understand they want to destroy me. But to persecute a harmless elderly couple to the point where they deliberately take their satchels and tablets, and they crawl on their hands and knees through a hole in a fence so as to be alone to Retire together? That's madness. It achieves nothing. How can the Department say it cares about us, then do that?"

"You know they'll be here soon, don't you?" she asked. "CommPol, I mean. The bench will have messaged them." He did not respond. Then she stepped round in front of him. "I have no rose to proffer," she said dropping to her knees. Before she could speak again, he followed her down and took her hands. "Co-Worker Gregor Workman 4978-88-915689734. This is me asking you. Will you marry me?"

He nodded. "Co-Medic Grete Steele, I can't remember your ID, but I am certain this is you, and this is me, answering you. As of this moment, we will consider ourselves married. Ceremonies can follow later. And my intention is that our marriage should last no less than 47 years, 2 months and 11 days."

She smiled, then hugged him. "You may want to start with a 7-year contract," she said as she drew him towards the exit of the RecArea. Outside, she hailed an Uber. As they climbed in and the vehicle hovered round the corner out of sight, the blue flashing light of a CommPol car came into the view of anyone who might have been standing by the RecArea. But at that hour of the morning, there was no one in the street to see it.

When they arrived home, Greg had recovered sufficiently to walk to the door without her support. As he dialled the entry code, his i-Comm bleeped. Inside, he checked the message, then wordlessly handed it to her to read:

The Departmental Republic v Co-Worker Gregor Workman 4978-88-915689734.

You are hereby informed that the date for your Preliminary Hearing has been set and is:

Redacted

A Departmental Attorney has been appointed to represent you. His contact details are:

Redacted

If you do not initiate contact with your Departmental Attorney within 48 hours of receipt of this i-Comm, it will be concluded that you wish to represent yourself at your forthcoming hearing.
The hearing will be held at

Redacted

Redacted

on
If you do not appear, the Tribunal will arrive at a preliminary conclusion on whether to forward your case to trial in your absence. Identiscan this i-Comm within 1 hour of receipt and return.

By order of the Department

Greg was back at work immediately following the next 8th day, but was increasingly prone to sitting inactive in front of his screen while his mind wandered. "My promotion has been postponed for no stated reason. I've been stripped searched without explanation. My parents have been driven to suicide. I've been accused of a crime but no one will tell me what I've done. I've been told that a date and location have been set for my preliminary hearing but no one will give me the details. I apparently have an appointed attorney, but no means of contacting him. There is nothing in any of the Departmental Life Manuals that covers this situation and I can think of no one I can turn to for help. It would appear that Compliance, passive Compliance is my only option. I am apparently expected to do nothing while events take their course. I'm quite sure they're out to destroy me, but why go about it in this way?"

At home, he wasn't sure whether to be profoundly grateful that he had Grete to confide in or deeply sorry for having drawn her into the chaos that his life was fast becoming. A month later, on day 9, two events occurred that further complicated matters. The 1ˢᵗ was that he received another i-Comm.

The Departmental Republic v
Co-Worker Greg Workman 4978-88-915689734.

You are hereby informed that your Preliminary Hearing has been held. Your decisions neither to attend nor to accept representation have been taken into account. The following date for your trial has been entered into the Diary of Central Court 4:

Redacted

You are advised that in the event of your nonattendance the trial will proceed without you and a verdict may be arrived at in your absence.

Confirm your receipt and understanding of the message by Identiprinting and returning it within 2 hours.

By order of Court 4.

The 2ⁿᵈ was that Grete informed him she was pregnant.

XIII

Greg anticipated that he would find it difficult to brief his Co-Workers without betraying his disdain for the procedures taking place under the water. As it happened, he had little opportunity anyway, for each group he spoke to resonated with the same questions about the Gill-Breathers. By the time he had answered questions from "Do they have procedures manuals we can study?" to "Do they use the toilets?" he repeatedly discovered he had little of the allotted time left to disseminate the planned information, anyway.

After 3 days of back-to-back presentations, he was exhausted. His own Permit Authorisation work was now a thing of the past. He barely had time to switch his screen on. Finally, at the end of day 3, 10 minutes before closedown time, he logged on to collect his messages. There was only 1 and it was from Tick, addressed to all members of the cluster group.

> *I want feedback on the debriefs you have undertaken with your colleagues. I shall, therefore, be holding 1-to-1 sessions with each of you. All meetings will be held in my office on floor 4 room 101. Inevitably, we will need to hold some of these meetings outside of normal office hours and for those of you involved, I have arranged Curfew Work Permits. Your time and date of meeting with me are stated below.*

He looked immediately to the end of the message. His meeting date was 3 days hence. His time was 20.00 hours. He winced. "I know the game she's playing," he thought. I can't let her win. "I can't let it happen again." But even as he did, somewhere inside, he was struggling to supress a part of himself that wanted a quite different outcome.

The screen notified him of its imminent switch off. He picked up his tablet, placed it in his satchel and filed out of the office with his Co-Workers towards the boats. Somewhere beneath the water, he knew a gong would be sounding, instructing the Fishpersons to cease work and swim home. "What is home to a Fishperson?" he wondered.

Greg slept through the whole Tram journey back to Suburbia, missing the comms link DepCasts. By the time he arrived at the LivUnit, he was fully anticipating Joe throwing himself through the doorway at him. But this time, he didn't. Greg entered the main room of the LivUnit to find his wife and son sitting in front of the SkypeWAll watching the closing moments of the 18.00 hours DepCast.

Grete turned to him. "What do you think?" she asked, an edge of uncertainty in her voice.

"What do I think of what?" he replied.

"The Department's going to flood more low lying land to make room for Gill-Breathers to come and live in 1stDep. They are calling it the New Occupied Territories and they're going to establish Gill-Breather settlements there.

What he replied was, "I'm sure if the Department believes it to be the right thing to do, then it will be fine." What he thought, and what he felt, was somewhat different.

By the time Greg returned home the following evening, Joe was back to his usual buoyant self. "Pop! Pop! There's going to be a Gill-Breather settlement 3 kilometres from our EdFac and Co-Educator Sam says we can go meet them with our parents. The Gill-Breather kids are so smart! They don't even have Compliance lessons. They breathe under water and play underwater games with special balls and... and..."

"Yes, Joe, I think I get the message."

"Can we go play with them, Pop? Can we? Can we, please? It would be really, really educational, Pop."

"I would think so, Joe," he had replied, wondering why he felt so uneasy about the prospect.

But in truth, his mind was elsewhere. His days were filled with debriefing Co-Workers on what he had seen on Waterfloor 1 and in the basement canteen. With each debrief, each repetition, Co-Workers became ecstatic at the perceived prospect of increased productivity. He was relieved that no one asked him what the point of the endless activity of the Fishpersons was that no one asked what benefit their repeated motions brought, or what was gained by their incessant reporting to the Sharkmen of *no change, no change, no change.*

In such thinking time as was available to him, Greg found his mind preoccupied with the forthcoming 1-to-1 session he was to have with Tick in her office. As the floor emptied at 17.00 hours on the day of his meeting, he busied himself with i-recording the notes that were supposed to be required for his debrief. He had little confidence that he would have opportunity to refer to them. At the approach of 20.00 hours, he climbed the stairs to the 4th floor, his heart rate increasing at the prospect of confrontation, for he was determined to resist this woman's unwanted advances, regardless of her seniority. The doors on the 4th floor landing swung back soundlessly at the pressure of his hand. The corridor behind them was in darkness. Sensing his motion, the lights brightened a little. Even in the low light of the night time setting, he could tell that the corridor was the same neutral grey as he recalled from higher up the building all those years ago, when he had failed to find room 101 on floor 7. Briefly, he wondered if he would be tested in the same way, whether floor 4 really contained a room 101 at all. The thought was expelled from his mind by the sight of a door just in front of him that was already ajar, a shaft of light shining though into the lower lit corridor. On the door was the number 101. He knocked.

"Come in, Co-Worker," called Tick. Greg pushed the door open wider to reveal a large, comfortably furnished office. At the far end of it, Tick was sitting behind a desk dictating into a screen. She looked up and smiled at him in a manner that betrayed nothing of any underlying intentions she might have for the evening. "Take a seat," she said, motioning to a meeting table at his end of the room. Its 6 places, each had a small screen built into the table surface facing up at 45°. Greg heard the door click shut behind him as he sat down. A moment later, Tick joined him, taking a seat on the opposite side of the table. "Thank you for staying late, Co-Worker, the Department is aware of the extra time you're making available."

"Anything for the Department that has done so much for me," Greg found himself saying automatically.

"And I must say, Co-Worker," she continued, "your contribution to the cluster group and the debriefs from Waterfloor 1 have been noticed and are appreciated." Greg smiled slightly and nodded.

"I know how hard this is for you, Greg." He sat back, startled. The last sentence had been spoken at little more than a whisper. "Perhaps you would like to start by talking me through your debrief seminars for the last 3 days." Her voice had returned immediately to normal.

He shook his head in slight confusion, then quickly reverted to normal. "Yes, of course. May I?" he asked motioning to the small screen in front of him. She nodded. And he turned it on, calling up his own work pages that contained his debrief notes. For the next 34 minutes, he delivered a less than enthusiastic summary of the 22 meetings he had held with Co-Workers, each a near exact repetition of the last. Tick listened throughout without interrupting him. Eventually, he stopped and looked at her enquiringly.

"Thank you, Co-Worker, that was thorough and most useful." It was an unambiguous, professional reply from a senior Co-Worker to a subordinate. Nothing more. Then, she sat looking at him, saying nothing. Greg waited for more from her but she did not oblige. She simply continued to sit and look at him. As the seconds grew into 1 minute, then 2, Greg became more and more uncomfortable as, in the absence of speech, the silence grew disturbing. Was she weighing up a professional issue? Was she about to move the encounter to the personal level that he emphatically did not want? What kind of game was she playing with him?

Eventually, he could stand the silence no longer. "Will there be anything else this evening, Co-Worker?" he enquired.

She raised her eyebrows. "*Will* there be anything else this evening, Co-Worker?" she parodied.

Momentarily, he was taken aback at the ambiguity she was imputing to his question. Recomposing himself and ignoring the meaning she had implied, he said, "Because if not, the hour is late and I should be getting home to my wife and son." He emphasised the last 3 words.

She was silent for some moments more. "Your wife and son," she said finally. "Yes, we know they are important to you. They would be, of course. And I know how hard you are finding this, Greg." Once more, the last sentence was delivered softly.

There it was again. The use of his 1st name, a reference to his personal life and the intonation in her voice. He shifted uncomfortably in his seat.

"I'm sorry, Co-Worker, I don't know what you're getting at," he said.

She looked at him again for several seconds, this time smiling sympathetically. "Poor Gregor," she said, but at normal volume this time, in a tone more indulgent than patronising. "There really is so much you don't know, isn't there? So very much you can only guess at, piece together from the little peeks you have been allowed of what lies underneath." She paused again. "Have you ever wondered what it would be like to know, rather than to guess, Greg? Do you ever think about what it would be like to be certain in your uncertainty about the certainty?"

He looked back at her, frowning in concentration, trying to squeeze the meaning from her enigmatic words, like pips from an overripe orange. He opened his mouth to speak, but she continued before he had a chance.

"I need to warn you," she said, her voice growing more serious, "that if we continue, there really is no going back. There can be no Cloud of Unknowing here. The fact is, you may prefer to remain in the comfort of ignorance. Many do, you know, certainly a majority. You may look back and regret this evening. But then again, perhaps regret is not what you're about. Perhaps your thirst for knowledge, for what you refer to as 'truth', overrides the dangers implicit in knowing. If we thought it otherwise, we would never have initiated this process with you. But you do need to remember, Greg. Pandora never had a box. She had a jar."

He was looking at her in total confusion now, utterly clueless about whatever it was she was talking about. Clouds, boxes, jars. What in JeKAllah's name was all this about? He wondered if she really knew herself.

"I can see you don't follow," she said in response to his expression. "Then let me tell you a story. A story from long, long ago, before there even was a Department."

Greg considered walking out, despite the fact that he lacked the authority or confidence to do so. It was only his old enemy, curiosity, that kept him in his seat.

"Zeus was father of all the gods," she continued, either not noticing his discomfort, or not caring.

"There is no other God than JeKAllah," Greg whispered under his breath, quoting the 1st line of the Universal Creed.

"Zeus and his wife Hura had a son, Hephaestus," she continued, ignoring his muttering. "Zeus ordered Hephaestus to create a woman, the 1st woman on all the earth. That woman was named Pandora."

"Then JeKAllah made a woman from the rib he had taken out of the man," quoted Greg quietly from the Universal Holy Book. "The woman's blasphemy is astonishing," he thought.

Again, Tick seemed not to notice the interjection and continued, "And Pandora was blessed. Oh, Greg, she was so blessed; as blessed as any woman could wish to be. Aphrodite bestowed her own beauty upon her, Athena endowed her with gifts of the finest clothing in all of Olympus and Hermes gave her speech. Oh, Greg! Her speech! Such soft, alluring words, such enticing tones, such penetrating insight. By that speech, and by her beauty, Pandora could have gained anything she could ever possibly have wanted from any man that would ever walk the earth. But Zeus, wily old Zeus! There was always a sting in the tail with Zeus. You'd do well to remember that when dealing with gods, Greg. Nothing is ever quite as it seems when you engage with us. Zeus gave Pandora a jar as a wedding gift, Greg, a *Pithos*, a jar as big as a man. And though she did not know it, the jar contained all the evils in the world, and yes, even death itself. And then, Greg, do you know what that wily old god did? He told Pandora never to open the jar!"

She stopped for a moment. Greg was silent now, captivated by her words, as if at that moment Tick was his own personal Pandora. And as he looked, he saw the tears forming in her eyes, reminding him of the day she had demonstrated the Oceanic Anthem with such obvious sincerity, "You can trust such sincerity," he found himself thinking.

"Greg, do you see it? Can you see that it was just too much temptation to place in front of any woman, any human? Zeus should never have done it. Humans need to be told what to do, what to think. They need boundaries, Greg. They need to understand that non-Compliance with the laws of the gods leads to death and destruction."

"What did Pandora do with the jar?" asked Greg, now engaged in the story despite himself.

"Isn't it obvious? She did what anyone would do when faced with such maddening uncertainty. She opened the jar, Greg."

"And what happened, then?" he asked.

"Surely, you can guess."

"Everything came out of the jar?" Greg guessed.

"Everything, except 1 thing."

"And what was that?"

"Hope. Only hope remained stopped up in the jar. And Greg, it has taken us almost 3,000 years to get that jar open again. 3,000 years to open it and to catch sickness, and death and misery and all the bad things that go with them. But we did it, Greg. We got all that evil back into Pandora's *Pithos* and we got the stopper back onto the jar. Can you see that, my lovely man? Can you see now, why we can't let you and the people like you take the stopper off the Pithos again? We simply can't take the risk of living another 3,000 years in misery."

Greg still didn't understand all she was saying, but he felt distinctly uncomfortable at being cast in the role of someone who would spread evil and destruction upon the earth. For that defined him as a Terrorist.

"We can't stop you thinking, of course. We never could. All we can do is offer you a decision." He looked at her enquiringly. "Only gods can be allowed to wield power, Greg. And only gods can be allowed to think freely. Your decision is whether you wish to join us on Mount Olympus. I-Comm your wife Greg, it's going to be a long night and you won't be going home. Come with me. We're leaving the office now. And while I think of it, it's time for you to start calling me Trish again."

"When did you recognise me?" he asked.

"The moment I 1st saw you. You've not changed much. When did you recognise me?"

"I didn't," he answered. "Not right up until the moment you told me. But you were 9 years and 4 months old when I last saw you, Trish. A girl of 9 years and 4 months changes a lot over the next 15 years."

She giggled. "I can imagine there are several things that are different about me now, Co-Worker. They were silent, then, for a while, the smoke from the spliffs curling up above them.

"Do you ever feel you're living inside a book?" he asked eventually.

"Everyone feels that, sometimes," she answered.

"No, I really mean it. Like my life has been planned. Like I'm following someone else's script in every action that I take."

"That's because you haven't broken free yet," she replied. "The true thinkers, those that shape our society, are the ones that have broken out of the script. When you're older, when you look back in years to come, you'll be able to see the opportunities you were given to break free. But only you can decide whether or not to take them. Most don't. Most prefer the security of the script – prefer the Department to do their thinking for them. The Department could never have survived if that were not the case. Only a few ever manage it."

"How so?" he asked.

"Some think independently. And it is those who pose the dilemma. So, we are forced to take a chance."

"What chance is that?"

"Why, the chance that once you have been given the chance to think independently, you'll not agree with us. The chance that you'll not side with the Department. We are at war, Greg, and if you are a thinker, you have to decide which side you're on."

"At war with the Terrorists and Vagrants, you mean?"

"No, not them. At least they're only a small part of what we are at war with."

"Well, you don't mean Eastasia and Eurasia, like in Nineteen Eighty-Four, do you?"

"No, they're Orwell's constructs. They don't exist. Or at least they don't exist in the form in which you're thinking of them. We are at war with entropy, Greg. We are at war with the tendency all things have towards disorder, towards deterioration, to the level of the lowest common denominator. Every society there has ever been, malevolent dictatorship, benevolent dictatorship, democracy, Babylon, Rome, Great Britain, The United States of America. You name it: every social system there ever was has fallen because of entropy in its social guise of disorder. Unless you confront entropy in its rawest form, it overtakes you; every time. And when the last sun in the last solar system in the last Galaxy burns out, it is entropy that will finally have won. Only Compliance stands against entropy, Gregor. Only universal conformity stands again universal disorder; and then, only for a season. The Department exists to fight the process of entropy for as long as possible. And the only way of doing that is through Compliance. Compliance makes as perfect a world as we can possibly have, for as long as we can have it."

He thought about her words before responding. "And what about freedom?"

"What kind of freedom would that be, Greg? The freedom of a

few to disrupt and destroy wantonly, or the freedom of the majority to live peaceful lives?"

"The right to a fair trial?" he asked, thinking back to the debacle of his own trial 15 years before.

"Oh, there are trials here, Greg, make no mistake about it. When we see something that needs dealing with, evidence is collated, considered and judged. The absence of advocates, the absence of a Terrorist or a Deviant from their own judgement does not mean that judgement is not exercised. Judgement is always exercised, a decision recorded and appropriate action taken."

"So, how do you ensure that the Department does not make a mistake when it exercises such 'appropriate action' following judgement?"

"We can't," she retorted. "But what legal system can? Centuries ago, there was trial by mob and execution by stoning. That was followed by trial by combat. You think these systems more reliable in arriving at fair judgement?"

"But what about – " he tried to interject, but she was in full flow and simply spoke over him.

"What about your precious trial by jury, the rule of law and the right of appeal? I can quote you a hundred examples or more over the last 200 years when that system went wrong, or was wilfully subverted by the authorities to get the result they wanted. From the hanging of innocents, through convictions for child abuse that turned out to be multiple death syndrome and rape convictions based on so-called suppressed memory syndrome, through to the deliberate misrepresentations in the service of political ends; time after time, your inaptly named 'freedom' and the so-called 'rule of law' has let down the individual, never mind the community. And if that's not enough, let's start on the list of murderers, terrorists, serial killers even, that were set free on technicalities to rape and murder and terrorise again. There are more of those than I can begin to tell you about. Yes, our system has its weaknesses. But are you really trying to tell me you want to return to the hit and miss vagaries of the way things were before? You're too intelligent for that, Greg. That is why we want you on the inside."

He was silent a while before answering.

"But how about freedom of choice?" he continued, "The freedom to do with our lives what we each choose to do."

"There are those that choose such *freedoms*," she answered carefully. "They find a way to leave our society, walking away in search of a dream. We used to try to stop them going. But you know what? We don't bother to now. Because they wander around in some Nowhereland, become cave dwellers living their malnourished lives on whatever they can trap or forage. And when they've discovered the misery that their dreams of freedom actually amount to, if they haven't died in the jaws of a wild animal, they try to return. That's when we stop them. They're diseased, Greg; some physically, for sure. But all, without exception, are mentally diseased. And we don't want that disease becoming an epidemic in our settled, happy society. Compliance, Greg; Compliance or social decimation. These are the only alternatives."

"And if I do?" he asked. "If I do side with the Department?"

"Then, Mount Olympus beckons – immediate Lev8 status and access to the world of the thinkers, the intelligentsia; an intellectual journey of discovery beyond any you have ever conceived of."

"I've never heard of Level 8," he replied.

"Oh, we have levels all the way up to 23. The thinker levels; the social engineers; the formers of belief; the creators of the trance of identity."

"What level are you Trish?" he asked.

She smiled but did not answer.

After fucking her a second time, when they were both lying on their backs, looking up at the Baroque ceiling of her bedroom, and the laser lights played with the smoke from their spliffs, he spoke again.

"And if I don't? If I don't side with the Department? If I don't agree that Compliance makes as perfect a world as can be achieved?"

"Then, there is room 101," she answered.

"Would that be room 101 where they hold birthday parties, or room 101 where the rats eat your face off?"

"Why not both?" she replied. Then she propped herself up on her right elbow and turned to look at him directly. "Can you see past the rats, Greg? Can you see past the birthday party? Can you understand what the metaphors stand for?"

He squirmed as an odd vision fleetingly crossed his mind of rats exploding from inside a birthday cake while candles burned serenely on the top.

"What happens after the birthday party?" she persisted. "What happens after the rats have eaten your face off? What then?"

"You die," he replied. "You die in the most horrible way conceivable."

She was silent for a moment, then said, "Old religion teaches us we must die in order to live."

"And if I do die? If I do blow out the candles and I do let the rats eat my face?"

"Then, room 101 contains everything you have ever wanted to see."

Greg's mind was filled with a vision of books, books as they had originally been written by the thinkers of the ages; a room where high walls were lined floor to ceiling with unadulterated knowledge, and still more books were piled up in towers and stacks all around him. "That's too easy," he said.

"Is it?" she asked. "Is it really so much easier to be egotistical? Is it really easy, that easy, to abandon all you've ever known for the sake of being a mismatcher, for the sake of mere information?"

"You were the one that said you were a god, not me."

She ignored the accusation. "I have to tell you, Greg, that if you do choose mismatching, there remains just one problem in room 101."

"And that is?"

She was silent for a moment. "Perhaps… perhaps I should not tell you. Perhaps it is something you need to discover for yourself."

"Tell me," he insisted.

"That's what I like to hear," she quipped. "The demand of one with true Compliance in his soul."

"You're evading the issue," he insisted. "Tell me what the problem is, in room 101."

She was silent again for a long time. So long, he was about to fuck her again. Then she spoke.

"The room is empty, Greg. It is a place of unadulterated loneliness. There are no human beings in room 101."

She had been wrong. He did return home that night, clutching tightly onto his Curfew Work Permit, along with his satchel and tablet. He had left her LivUnit quietly when she had finally fallen asleep, walking out past the empty wine bottle that she had opened when they had arrived, their glasses now on the cabinets next to her bed. He had let himself out onto the 42nd floor of a tower block he had never visited and taken the lift down to water level. The block had its own dedicated boats and boatmen working 24 hours a day who ferried him out to the dry land dock without question. From there, he had taken an Uber home, where he had let himself silently into his own LivUnit. Then, pushing his duplicity as far behind him as he could reach, he had undressed and slid into bed, next to his wife's warm sleeping body, with all the familiarity and comfort and all that Compliance it represented. But though she was just centimetres from him he could not reach out to her, he could not approach her for cause of the ravine he had opened up between them. Pulling the duvet over him, he stared at the ceiling, as alone as if he were alone, and wondered whether he wanted to become a god, or whether the simple pleasure of ignorant Compliance called louder to him than the siren voice of knowledge ever could.

XIV

It took only 1 month and 5 days before the Department announced that the Gill-Breather colony was established and could be visited. Joe had talked of little else during that time, whittling away at any latent resistance his father might have harboured against taking him to visit the Fishpersons at the earliest opportunity. "Well, if we're going," he had said to him, "you're going to need to hold your breath under water, and that takes practice." Greg had taken Joe and Grete through the exercises that the cluster group had undertaken at work, showing them how to slow their heart rates and gradually increasing their lung capacities. Meanwhile, he had registered his family for the 1st organised visit to the colony. What he did not voice, even to himself, was the fact that the project gave him a focus, something to work on with Joe and thus, an opportunity to avoid honest discussion with Grete.

On the agreed 8th day morning, they assembled with a group of 42 other adults and excited children, including some from Joe's EdFac, for a final briefing at a newly constructed Jetty at the edge of the New Occupied Territories. While his parents listened carefully to their final instructions, Joe was paying more attention to his new wetsuit. Then, in groups of 4, 5, or 6, they dived into the water under the guidance of a group leader. There was never a dive on which Greg was not grateful for the certainty that he would soon return to the surface. He looked around carefully as his family swam down towards the settlement. The infrastructure was little changed from the time that the area had been open to the air. Roads, LivUnits, gardens, all were still in place as before. But now the population moving around were the Gill-Breathers. He watched as Grete looked on at their activities with a somewhat detached expression on her face, almost as if she were visiting a zoo or museum. Joe, for his part, was a picture of blissful excitement. But most noticeable of all to Greg were the activities of those they had come to observe.

All around, life was continuing in a parody of normality. For the creatures were enacting, as far as they could, life as it would be lived above the surface. A vehicle propelled by some unknown power source passed them containing a Fishperson family, only to circle around and return. Children with fish heads were playing with a football that had to be dropped in slow motion from one child to the other. But to Greg's now experienced eye, the fish-children played like automatons, seemingly doing what they thought they were supposed to do in a parody of play whose counterpart above the surface would have been instinctive. Other Fishpersons pegged washing on lines where it swayed in the current of the water. In each direction he turned, Greg saw the Sharkmen strategically placed, as if to prevent the Fishpersons from swimming out of a designated area. He peered into windows where family groups gathered around inoperable SkypeWAlls, seemingly imitating the patterns they would have enacted if they had been dry land dwellers. But while others in the observer groups marvelled at the creatures' ability to breathe under water, Greg was overwhelmingly conscious of the universal lack of spontaneity.

The group leader signalled to Greg's family that it was time to leave. With thankfulness that he did not have to stay, Greg broke surface to a single thought that had never occurred to him before: had these strange, unnatural creatures once been human?

He did not have long to consider the matter, for as soon as they had returned to the jetty, Joe was all over him. "Oh, Pop! It was amazing! Did you see the fish-children playing with the football?

That was incredible! And did you see the families in the houses, Pop? Did you see them? Weren't they just... just amazing! I wish I could be a Fishperson, Pop. Can we dive again, Pop? Can we? Can we dive again, pleeease?"

Greg was relieved there were no second dives available, due to pressure of interest from the many that were curious to observe the Fishpersons at 1st hand. Grete sat quietly on the journey home, deep in thought. For his part, Joe didn't stop talking about what he had seen. It wasn't until they actually walked through the front door of their own LivUnit that the thought came to Greg: they had observed the Gill-Breathers with immense interest. Why had the Gill-Breathers shown no interest in them?

XV

The smoke curled up to the ceiling, breaking the illusion that it had a dome. The angels and cherubs continued to stare down. Greg wondered if they were sitting in judgement or simply being thoughtful. "Nothing is what it seems, is it?" he said.

"That's a little deep for me, today," she replied, the fingers of her right hand lightly stroking his inner thigh.

"No, I mean it," he persisted." Take work. All the nonsense about Permit Authorisation when we all know that a Permit Application has never, within the collective living memory of all of us, ever been rejected."

"Want to know a secret?" she asked.

"Yes," he said, irritation seeping through in the tone of his voice. It irked him that she knew so much and he so little.

"You're right. No permit has ever been rejected. And you want to know why? Because no genuine application has ever been submitted." He snorted his disapproval. "And how about this," she continued. "On the other side of the City from the Permits Authorisation building is another building. It houses the Permits Applications Section. Same size as your Section, same layout, same organisational structure. But there, the Lev1s and 2s create Permit Applications from information we feed through to their screens. They are 100% sample checked by Lev 6ers and 7ers who've spent their entire career working their way up in the Section. Then, when we're absolutely sure they are correct, we ship the Applications over to your building for your Section to authorise."

"What utter crap," he responded.

"The best is still to come," she replied. "Because for all those applications, for all the work undertaken creating and checking them, no one ever travels anywhere."

"How do you know all this?"

"Because I am responsible for both buildings, Greg. Both sections are under my personal control."

"And this is what the gods of Olympus spend their immortal lives doing? This is the intelligentsia you want me to join?" Her hand moved to his scrotum, the pressure increasing a little. He shuddered. "The work is not as pointless as it looks. Everything we do is purposeful. You ought not to be so judgemental until you have the information necessary to form an opinion."

"And the purpose is?" he asked.

"Think about it," her hand continuing to massage him. "Think about the number of educated individuals our universities turn out each year. And each generation of graduates is a little more educated than the last. You have a single PhD. It's virtually unheard of now to leave university with less than 2. And all those people have to be given work, or they become discontented."

"Can't they do something more useful than stamping Permits? Can't they… make things or something?"

"When was the last time you met someone who makes anything? All production is automated now. AI systems control the factories. All distribution is bot-driven. But people still need to feel their lives are purposeful. So, we invent work to keep them occupied."

"How utterly pointless."

"In my opinion, no. After all, the purpose of work is to fulfil us, is it not? Who do you know from your neighbourhood, or at work, or anywhere else who would say they are unfulfilled? In the whole of our society, the only people, regardless of education, regardless of intellectual ability, who are not fulfilled are the mismatchers – people like you, Greg."

"And when people like me begin to question what's going on?"

"We, err, stimulate them," she replied.

He closed his eyes. "So, all that happened to me 15 years ago, the room 101 stuff, the disciplinary, the 'Trial': all that was just *stimulation*?"

"In a manner of speaking, yes."

"Including the suicide of two harmless, innocent elderly people."

She waited a moment before answering. "It wasn't supposed to happen like that," she said. "The Watch Officers who searched your LivUnit were... inexperienced; excessively enthusiastic. They were disciplined."

"It gives me great comfort to know that," he replied sarcastically, swinging his legs away from her and over the edge of the bed. Then he sat with his back to her, reliving yet again the night of his parents' death. Finally, he stood, still facing away from her.

"Come back, Greg. Let me make you feel better."

He hesitated, still not facing her. "You know, I'm not at all sure I want to be a god," he said.

"Be careful, Greg," she replied, a note of warning entering her tone. "Zeus is growing impatient. Olympus will not be open to you for ever."

"Olympus doesn't sound like home to me. There has to be a home for other gods."

"There is only room 101," said Trish. "And remember, Greg, *Whom the gods would destroy, they 1ˢᵗ make mad.*"

He did not turn when he replied. "Perhaps, I'll take my chance on madness."

He returned home on mental autopilot that evening, going through all the necessary motions while his thoughts were engaged elsewhere. Grete greeted him with news from work. The MedFac had been instructed to prepare itself for mass operations; day cases only, for the procedure was straightforward. The whole population was to be offered gill implants. More of 1ˢᵗDep, much more, was to be flooded. The DepCasts would be made the next day. Joe was ecstatic at the prospect of being able to make friends with the fish-children.

That night, he turned and turned, failing to sleep. "Whom the gods would destroy," he thought. "Whom the gods would destroy…"

Eventually, still fully awake, he sat up and looked at Grete sleeping calmly beside him. "Sleep in heavenly peace," he whispered, quoting from *Universal Spiritual Songs*. Sadly, he reached out and placed a hand on her shoulder, shaking her gently awake. She blinked up at him in the half-light, making her way back from whatever peaceful dream she had been enjoying.

"There's something I need to tell you," he said.

XVI

It was an overwhelmingly happy moment and he really did try to be happy. But the thought of bringing a child into the world at this time, of all times? And so soon after the untimely death of his parents? The joy that this would otherwise have given them served only to underline the sadness of the moment. Greg had done all the right things to convey to Grete his delight at the news – rushed to make her sit down, made her tea, asked to listen against her belly for signs of the baby's presence. Despite the seriousness of his predicament, she had laughed 'til her sides ached, a laughter that despite himself he found overwhelmingly infectious. And they had sat on the sofa holding each other and laughing and crying, neither of them entirely sure how much of the emotion was joy, how much sadness and how much was hysteria born of fear.

Finally, she had asked to see the i-Comm again. She had read it closely, then looked at him seriously. "I don't want to raise your hopes unnecessarily," she said. "But I'm wondering if Central Court 4 might be in Admin District 4?"

The next 8ʰ day, they took an Uber to Admin District 4, alighting into an empty street. As the taxi backed soundlessly away, they looked up at the forbidding high rise buildings towering all around them, so busy on a working day, but deserted on an 8ʰ Day. Greg began to walk away from Grete, when she grabbed his arm. "Look," she said, pointing. His eye followed the direction of her arm. 200 metres away stood a smaller, less imposing building than the others. Judging by its architecture it was older than any other building on the street. It stood only 3 storeys above ground, long and squat, looking dwarfish against its soaring neighbours. Unlike a modern Admin building, it had windows all around it at regular intervals. Strangely, none were bricked up, though several were boarded, giving the impression that it was semi-derelict. Over the centre rose a pillared dome on top of which stood a squat tower. The tower was topped by a statue of a woman with her arms stretched out at right angles from her body as she stood upon a globe. In one hand was an ancient weighing scale. The other was empty, though it might well have held something once, long ago. The woman's eyes were bandaged, as if she were blind. The statue had evidently once been covered with gold leaf or paint, most of which had long since worn away. "Makes you glad of eye implants, doesn't it?" said Grete as they approached.

Greg stopped, gripping her hand. "Look!" he said pointing. On the wall by the side of the door stood a sign. It said 'Central Court 4.' "We've found it," he whispered. He ran to the door and immediately gripped the knocker with both hands, rapping it hard onto the door,. The sound echoed back to him from inside the empty building.

He knocked again. And he kept on knocking until Grete gently placed her hand onto his and said, "That's enough, Greg. I don't think there's anyone here today. We'll have to come back on a working day." It was at that moment a voice emanated from within the building.

"Who seeks entry to the Court?" it said.

Greg looked at Grete in surprise. She smiled broadly and prodded him. "Go on," she said. "Answer him."

Greg turned back to the door. "Gregor Workman, 4978-88-915689734. This is me," he said. "Can you let me in, please?"

A moment later, the sound of drawing bolts followed. Eventually, the door swung back, squeaking on its unoiled hinges. Inside was a very large lobby, surprisingly well illuminated, with daylight streaming down from the windows of the dome onto the remains of a large patterned marble floor. Greg just had time to see how badly damaged and neglected the floor was, when the voice spoke again from behind the door. "The Court grants you access, Greg Workman, 4978-88-915689734, if this is you. But if you do not enter now, this door will close and you cannot be sure it will ever open to you again."

He needed no second warning. Taking Grete's hand, he stepped through the doorway and onto the uneven floor. He was just able to see how much of the beautiful marble had been wantonly looted before the sound of the door being bolted behind him made him turn again.

In a moment, his hope that he had finally found a way out of the ludicrous bureaucratic maze faded. Before him stood a man in late middle age, overweight and sweating, leaning heavily on a cane and breathing with obvious difficulty. Even allowing for the man's stoop, his height could not have been more than 150 centimetres. He wore thick horn-rimmed spectacles and on his head he wore a long, plaited wig that would never fool anyone into believing it was his own hair. He was dressed in a full-length red robe edged in what appeared to be animal fur that had once been white. Large cuffs of similar dirty white fur edged the sleeves. Below the robe, the lower parts of his legs were visible, clothed in black stockings that ended in black shoes with tarnished gold buckles. In the hand that he did not use to lean on the cane, he carried a large mop and a bucket of dirty water.

The man squinted at Greg through his spectacles. "What do you want?" he asked. "Can't you see I'm busy?"

Greg held out his i-Comm, already displaying the message about his court date.

"Can you tell me, please," he asked, trying to sound respectful, "am I in the right place and do you know anything about this?"

"My Lord."

"I'm sorry?" replied Greg.

"My Lord," repeated the man. "You call me, 'My Lord.' I am a High Court judge of the 498th Division and I am entitled to be referred to as 'My Lord'. Unless, that is, you want to be found in contempt of court."

"Err, My Lord," said Greg, correcting himself quickly, "Can you please tell me anything about this?" He was still holding out his i-Comm.

The High Court judge squinted down at the screen. "Yes, what about it?" he replied, looking back up at Greg.

"My Lord, can you please tell me if I'm in the right place and if you know anything about this communication."

"Right place? What does it say on the door?"

"Err, Central Court 4, My Lord."

"And what does it say on your toy?"

It took Greg a moment to realise the judge was referring to the i-Comm.

"It says my case is being tried in Court 4, My Lord."

"Then why the Devil are you asking me if you're in the right place? Can't you see I'm busy? I've got floors to mop, don't you know?"

Greg felt elated and confused and doubtful all at the same time.

"Thank you, My Lord. And, err, can you tell me anything about it please?"

"Tell you anything about it? Certainly," replied the judge. "I'm responsible for all the cleaning here as well as trying the cases. Not that there are many of those nowadays. What do you want to know about mopping floors? Have they sent you to help me?"

"I'm sorry, My Lord," replied Greg. "I meant, can you tell me anything about this message, please?"

"The message on your toy, you mean?" replied the judge. "Of course, I can tell you about it. I wrote it, didn't I? What do you want to know, Gregor Workman, 4978-88-915689734?"

Greg had to lean on Grete's shoulder to stop himself collapsing in relief.

"Oh," he said. "Oh, My Lord. I'm so relieved to have found you. It's about the trial."

"Trial? What trial?" asked the judge. "Is there going to be a trial? We've not had one of those for years."

"Well, that's the problem, My Lord. It doesn't say."

"Doesn't say?" replied the judge. "Preposterous. Of course it says. How would you know when to come if it didn't say? Give it here."

Wordlessly, Greg handed the i-Comm back to the judge who squinted at the screen again through his horn-rimmed spectacles. "Well, it doesn't say when the trial is, does it? So how do you know when to come?"

Greg cleared his throat. "My Lord, that's my problem. I don't know when to come for the trial."

The judge snorted. "Nonsense. We have procedures for that. We send you a message. Haven't you had a message telling you you're on trial?"

Greg remained calm only with a struggle. "I've had this message, My Lord. Only this message."

"Well, come when it says in the message to come," answered the judge.

"I can't," shouted Greg, finally losing his composure. "The message doesn't say when to come!"

"Damn i-Comms," said the Judge. "It was much easier when we had e-mail." He looked at his wrist. On it was an antique watch. "Can do it now if you like?" he suggested, looking up at Greg. "Just got time before I have to finish the floors."

"Yes! Yes!" replied Greg, afraid the judge might change his mind if he did not respond immediately.

"Right, come this way," said the judge. "And bring your pretty lawyer with you," he continued, nodding at Grete.

Greg looked at Grete, who was looking back doubtfully. "Don't say anything," he hissed. "Just do as the silly old fool says. There's half a chance we might finally be getting somewhere with this."

The judge led them towards a pair of double doors to one side of the large derelict lobby. "This courtroom will do." He pushed on the door. Nothing happened. "Bah! Forgotten my damn key, haven't I?" he mumbled in Greg and Grete's general direction. "Sorry, can't proceed today."

Greg winced.

"Isn't there somewhere else we can hold the trial, My Lord?" asked Grete.

"What's that you say, young lady?" retorted the judge. "You'll have to speak up. Forgotten my hearing aids today."

Greg thought of prosthetic inner ear implants, but refrained from mentioning them.

"I said isn't there somewhere else we can hold the trial, My Lord?" repeated Grete, much louder.

"Somewhere else? That's a good idea," replied the judge. "Where do you suggest?"

"Is there another courtroom, My Lord?"

"Another courtroom, you say?" said the judge, leaning in towards Grete rather too closely for her personal comfort. "Good idea, young lady. You'll go far in the legal world. Tell you what, let's use that one," he said, pointing across the hall. "I left it open when I went to answer the door. Was there anyone at the door, by the way?" Grete didn't respond. "Damn kids," continued the judge. "Always playing knock-down-Ginger. I'd knock 'en down if I could catch 'em."

"The, err, courtroom, My Lord," said Grete, nodding to the open door on the other side of the lobby.

"Yes. I've had a really good idea. Let's use that one for the trial." And he strode off faster than Greg would have thought him capable, cane in one hand, mop and bucket still in the other. Nor did the judge slacken his pace when they entered the courtroom, for he marched purposefully towards a large red chair on a dais at the far end. "You sit there," he called back to Grete and Greg, pointing towards the fixed bench seating in front of the dais. As he reached the large chair, he said, "All rise, Court is now in Session. The honourable... the honourable... Damn. Forgotten my name. An honourable judge of the High Court presiding. Let all persons who have business with the court approach and they will be heard."

At the instruction, 'All rise', Greg and Grete immediately stood up. The judge peered down at them. "Which of you is the Defendant and which is the Representative?"

"I am the Defendant, My Lord," replied Greg.

The judge squinted down at Greg and frowned. "If you're the Defendant, get in the damn dock!" he shouted, pointing to his left. Greg scrambled past Grete and climbed the stairs to the dock as quickly as he could. "Are you dangerous?" the judge asked.

"Err, no, My Lord," replied Greg, "not dangerous."

"Right. Let me know if you get dangerous and I'll have you shackled."

"Yes, My Lord," replied Greg.

"Right you," said the judge pointing to Grete. "If you're the representative, why are you improperly dressed? Why haven't you got a wig on?"

Grete thought quickly. "I gave it to you outside the courtroom, My Lord. You'd forgotten your own and asked to borrow mine. You do remember, don't you?"

"Remember? Of course I remember, young woman. What do you think I am? Forgetful or something? Now, let's get on with the case. What's your client accused of?"

"If you please, My Lord, we have not been informed."

"Not informed? Preposterous. Where's the Prosecution?"

"If it please the Court, My Lord, the Prosecution hasn't turned up for the trial."

"Please the Court?" snorted the judge. "Please the Court? Don't be ridiculous, young woman. Of course it doesn't please the Court. It's a damn waste of the Court's time when I should be mopping floors."

"I do understand, My Lord," replied Grete, trying to sound sympathetic, "how valuable the Court's time is. In the absence of the Prosecution representative or even an accusation, might I propose that the case is dismissed? Then, you can get back to washing the floors."

"Dismissed, you say? Yes, interesting idea. I shall consider my verdict. Wait here, both of you. And you," he said, nodding to Greg, "are you sure you're not dangerous? It would be no trouble to shackle you, you know. You only need to ask. I'm pretty influential round here."

"Err, thank you, but no, My Lord," said Greg trying to keep a straight face. "Not dangerous at all, My Lord."

"All rise," instructe, the judge, standing up. But both Greg and Grete were already standing. The judge exited the courtroom by a door adjacent to his seat. Greg looked at Grete and shrugged his shoulders. She sat down. From behind the dais they heard the sound of an old-fashioned lavatory being flushed. It was all they could do to keep themselves from bursting out laughing.

122

A moment later, the judge returned to the courtroom. "All rise," he said as he took his seat. Grete stood. 'Court in session," said the judge. He made no reference to who was presiding. "Right," he said, "let the Prosecution commence its case." Greg and Grete both groaned inwardly.

"Err, if it please the Court, My Lord, the Prosecution has failed to appear for the trial and we are requesting dismissal of the case."

"Oh. Yes. That's right. I remember now. Yes. Case dismissed. Defendant is free to go. Does anyone have a bucket of hot water, please?"

They arrived back that the LivUnit still in fits of laughter and leaning on each other for support. "It's just as well you remembered to get him to Identiprint the verdict," said Greg having recomposed himself. "By tomorrow, he will have forgotten the whole thing ever happened."

That night in bed, after making love, Greg finally started to allow himself to feel better. His parents were gone and nothing was going to bring them back. But the court had finally pronounced him a free man, and he was here holding the woman he loved, who was carrying their 1st child. Greg felt his broken life was beginning to heal.

"Have you thought what to call her?" he asked softly, his arms wrapped around Grete.

"Call who?" she asked.

"Our daughter."

"We're not having a daughter. Our 1st child will be a boy. We can have a daughter after that. We have plenty of time."

"All right," he had replied. "Have you thought about what to call him?"

"Frank," she answered. "His name is Frank."

They lay silently, so lost in the warmth of love and happiness that they barely noticed the bleep of her i-Comm. She reached out a sleepy hand to the bedside cabinet and drew the device back to her, reading it under the duvet. Then, Greg heard her moan; a long, guttural moan that turned into a growl and then a shriek that ended in a long piercing scream. She leapt from the bed and ran naked through the LivUnit and out of the front door, where she dropped to her knees in the front garden, still screaming. He followed her about two seconds later.

"What is it?" he yelled in terror as he knelt by her in the front garden. "What's happened?"

"i-Comm," she managed to gasp, pointing back into the house still moaning and holding her belly. Greg stormed back into the LivUnit and into the sleeping partition, then tore the duvet off the bed in search of Grete's i-Comm. The message was still on screen as she had left it.

Suburbia MedFac22 to Grete Steele 5151-88-915689734

It has been reported that you have permitted yourself to become impregnated without having applied for a permit for Nuclear Living Group Expansion. You will report within 24 hours of receipt of this communication to the above Medical Facility for immediate termination of your unauthorised pregnancy.

If this is you, return your Identiprint immediately in confirmation of receipt of this message.

Greg dropped involuntarily to his knees, hyperventilating. Then he threw the i-Comm at the wall, where it shattered, spreading shards all over the bed.

It was his turn to scream.

XVII

The ceiling looked different from here, seated upright, fully clothed. She had answered the door in an untied negligée, had tried to take him straight into her arms and kiss him. He had put his hands up to stop her. He watched her take a step back, watched as her expression changed from warm and welcoming to harsh and cautious.

"What's the problem?" Trish had asked. He had told her of his conversation with Grete the previous night: how she had listened in silence as he disclosed his infidelity, neither screaming at him nor crying, evaluating his words carefully, as if he were a medical subordinate making a professional report to her. And he had, indeed, felt like a subordinate, like he was less than her now: low, and beneath her, for she occupied all the high places, the laudable, esteemed noble places that existed in his world. At the end of his long explanation, his confession, she had turned to him.

"Are you leaving us?" Grete had asked.

He had shaken his head. "No, not if you still want me. I've come to my senses. I have learned the value of what I have." He had reached for her then, but she had pulled away, drawing the covers over her, turning her back to him.

"I don't know, Greg. I need to think this through. And now, I need to sleep. I have work in the morning." He had marvelled at the coolness of her response, at her ability simply to sleep after what he had told her.

"So, are you leaving me?" Trish asked him, lighting a spliff, her 1st of the day.

"Leaving?" he replied. "That would imply I have actually been

125

with you in any meaningful sense. I don't think I have, certainly not emotionally."

She drew sharply on the cigarette and shook her head. "Not that it matters," she said, breathing the smoke outwards and upwards. "I knew you'd decided not to join us and I've already told you what the consequences would be."

"Rats or candles?" he asked, facetiously.

"Maybe neither, maybe both," she answered. "But as it happens, matters have moved faster than we had anticipated. The non-Compliance has grown further than anyone expected it to, so we're completing the flooding today. We'll finish the operations from under water if we have to."

"Gill implants?" he asked.

She shook her head. "No. It's been decided, we move straight to prosthetic fish heads. It's the final solution to achieving complete Compliance. That's what we learned from the Oceanic Union. It's for that technology we needed to merge with them. Everyone below Lev8 will become Fishpersons. It's definitely for the best for everyone. So, you'd better go home and enjoy what time you have left with your family. In a few days, they'll not know who you are, nor you, them."

He paused for just a moment, questioning whether she was serious or not. "You're mad," he said. "You're all utterly insane." Then, he turned and fled, banging his palm repeatedly on the lift call button on the wall just outside her apartment. Once on the water, he stood at the prow of the boat as it ferried him to the jetty, then jumped onto the landside and ran. Greg ran as fast as he had run on the night Neighbourhood Watch had followed him. He ran as if he had just 2 minutes 58 seconds to get home. At the City Transport Terminal, he leapt onto a Tram as the doors were closing, checking the time, counting the stops, counting the seconds as they ticked his life, his family's life away. As the Tram drew into the

Suburbia Terminal, he forced its doors open with his bare hands before it had settled to the ground and leapt half a metre down onto the platform. Then he had run to the LivUnit at the same speed as he had run at the city end; up the street, through the garden gate and up the front path. Then he stopped. The door was open, fully recessed into the wall. On the white-wall itself were spray painted the words 'Room 101' in bright red letters. Greg roared "No," then leapt through the open door to find himself wading through 3 centimetres of water. The taps in the Nutriprep area were on full flow. Sewage gurgled up through the toilet. Oblivious to it all, he searched the LivUnit room by room. His family, his precious family were gone and so were their satchels and tablets.

Greg ran back out through the open door, turning 1st, one way, then the other, not knowing which direction they had taken. Outside in the street, the manhole covers were lifting off the sewers as the sewage rose under them and the street mains were bursting with the pressure of the water inside them. Not knowing where else to go, he ran towards Grete's MedFac, which was next door to Joe's EdFac. But when he arrived, both buildings had been abandoned and the doors were wide open, medical and educational detritus littering the floors. Greg ran back out, then stopped, bent double and howled as behind him the distant high-rise blocks deluged from every window of every floor as the streets flowed like rivers.

He turned for home again, in the hope that Grete and Joe might have been able to get back to the LivUnit. Hordes of panicking people were half running, half swimming past semi-submerged vehicles, while others frantically built makeshift barriers out of any materials to hand, in vain attempts to keep the rising water out of their LivUnits. A few, the 1st of many, Greg had thought, had simply sat down on walls or park benches, opened their satchels and taken their tablets. The lifeless bodies remained where they were, or floated downstream in the rising current.

Greg arrived home, hoping in desperation that his family would have returned. But the LivUnit was still empty. Finally, he stopped, pulled an upright chair from the dining table and sat down. The 1st calm thought that came to him was that now, at this moment, he would open the *Pithos* if he could, and risk releasing all the negativity, if only he could also release hope. But the 1st thought was followed by a 2nd. How could he possibly open the jar when the Department had already done so? In the name of the war on Entropy, they had opened it and once again released death and destruction upon the world, and all in pursuit of some fictitious, unattainable ideal of Compliance. In his delirious anger, a *Pithos* shimmered into existence in the corner of the room. Greg roared and lunged forward, grabbing at the jar that was as big as he was. With all his strength, he turned it over and shook it and shook it and shook it. But there was nothing more to come out. Zeus had lied. In 3,000 years, hope had never resided in that jar. Greg lifted it high, high above his head and threw it as far as he could. It flew out over the LivUnits that were slowly disappearing under the water, out over the Tower Blocks and beyond. On and on flew the jar, powered only by the force of his rabid anger, towards Mount Olympus, smashing at the feet of Zeus and his brigand hoard of lunatic deities. And as Greg watched it splinter into a thousand shards at the feet of the apoplectic god, for a moment, the briefest of nanoseconds, he felt satisfaction. Oh, it was so good to feel anything again, anything that defined him as human. But the moment passed and the feeling sank back into the amorphous numbness of his soul as Greg returned to reality where the waters continued to rise.

Despairing of looking for Grete and Joe any longer, he took refuge in the boarded loft of his LivUnit, lining it with plastic sheeting and gluing the sheets together with welding compound. As the waters finally lapped at the loft hatch, he climbed inside, still weeping for his lost family that he had so foolishly discarded. He had no way of knowing how long the air would last or whether the roof would take the pressure of the water rising above him. He really didn't care.

It was more than 48 hours later that he was driven out by thirst and hunger. His only exit was the loft hatch, for by now, Greg could hear that the waters had risen above the level of the roof and only the welded plastic sheets were keeping the air in. He took a deep breath and dived into the LivUnit, where his family's sodden possessions floated eerily around him in the swirling current. He tried not to look, tried not to extract memories from the ruined objects that represented a life he knew had gone forever. He 1st retrieved some bottled water and canned food from the Nutriprep area and returned to the loft to consume them. Then, he swam down again, exiting the house by the open front door. He was prepared for darkness in the waters outside, but light was still reaching street level from the surface above him. And in the 7 minutes of airtime that he had to take in the scene around him, Greg was confronted by sights he could only describe as surreal.

All around, life was continuing in a grotesque parody of normality. For in the short time of his absence, men and women and children had become Gill-Breathers, taking on the characteristics of marine life, yet retaining in their behaviour some echo of their former humanity. On the dive into the New Occupied Territories, Greg and his family had watched these creatures, half fish, half human, drive in aimless circles around children with fish tails playing with footballs that had to be dropped in slow motion. He remembered Fishpersons pegging washing on lines where it swayed in the current of the water, and family groups gathered in front of inoperable SkypeWAlls. Now, he came upon a SocEngage where more Fishpersons stood in groups at a bar, raising litre glasses full of water to their mouths, while a publican Fishperson ritually polished glasses full of water with a waterlogged cloth. All around his home, the formerly human Gill-Breathers Compliantly repeated the patterns they had enacted out of choice when they were dry land dwellers. The difference now was that there was no spontaneity anywhere, no laughter, no joy, no pain, and certainly, no tears. All acted as if programmed, controlled by some hideous group-shoal-mind, endlessly repeating the normal acts of daily life as if nothing had changed, as if they were still as human as they had once been. And everywhere he looked, Greg saw the mindless, silent mouthing, in parody of communication, from those who had nothing to say. Eventually, his lungs all but bursting, he returned to his loft, thankfully gulping down lungful after lungful of life-preserving air. He had never been so grateful in all of his life for air – but more so for his humanity.

The following morning, Greg woke with water lapping at his face. Choking, and with his rib cage all but collapsing, he leapt instinctively upwards towards the sloping roof of his loft, where he gulped at the remaining air trapped in the apex. He took the deepest breath he could and dived through the loft hatch.

Still more unexpected sights confronted him. Outside, gill-breathing shoals of commuter Fishpersons were swimming down the pavement in groups marshalled by Sharkmen, Each Fishperson carried a satchel in hand. Greg wondered if they contained some Fishperson version of tablets. In unison, they habitually checked their inoperable i-Comms, as if seeking to reassure themselves they would arrive on time for some phantom Transporter departure for the City that now would never take place. Greg followed, stopping at air pockets in abandoned cars, bus shelters and anywhere else they remained. Instinct told him to keep himself as concealed as he could. It did not take long for him to realise how well that instinct was serving him. As he proceeded further and further towards the city, he watched in revulsion as shoals of Sharkmen systematically cornered the few remaining air breathers who had survived. Without warning or mercy, they tore into their victims' flesh in horrific blood fests, their soundless screams of the dying sculpted into their terrified faces.

Packed densely together for protection, the City-bound shoals swam determinedly forward under the unforgiving fish-eyes of the Sharkmen, arriving at their water-covered buildings at precisely 9.00 am. Greg had no need to follow any further. He knew exactly how these mindless creatures would be spending their day. As he watched through the window of a waterlogged building, his thoughts returned to the question of whether he would ever again see his family. It was then he turned to find his way blocked by four Sharkmen. Greg looked in every direction, including up and down, but it was obvious to him that there could be no escape. He was about to give himself over to a bloody fate when to his surprise, the Sharkmen closed in around him and ushered him up to the surface where he emerged, gulping gratefully at his 1st fresh air in days. From a building-side jetty, a hand reached down to help him from the water.

Instinctively he stretched out his arm and grabbed it, levering himself out of the water and the reach of the unpredictable jaws that hovered below. "I wasn't quite certain I'd be seeing you again," said Trish matter-of-factly. "But now that you're here, there's someone I want you to meet – again." His hopes rose. Could it be that she had found and saved Grete and Joe?

Trish led him into the building, which was unknown to Greg, by a recently constructed waterside entrance. He glanced upwards, estimating that perhaps 30 or 40 storeys remained above the water. There were probably the same number below. Inside the building, walls, floor and ceiling were Departmental grey. There was no furniture in sight and no security screening. "But why would there be," thought Greg, "We're 30 or more floors up from yesterday's entrance level." Trish pressed the lift button. Evidently the system had been modified to work in water as well as in air, for according to the floor indicator above the doors, the car was rising to them from beneath. Trish ushered him inside. "Floor 77," she instructed.

They exited the lift onto a landing indistinguishable from the one they had left on the water level floor below, other than for the entrance that had been constructed at water level. "In through there please," said Trish, nodding towards a pair of swing doors. Greg looked for surveillance cameras, for entry controls, but could see none.

"Where are we going, Trish?" he asked.

She maintained her disdainful expression. "I would have thought you'd be able to guess that by now," she replied.

He nodded. "Room 101?" he asked.

"Eventually. Somewhere else 1st," she responded.

"Are we actually going to find Room 101 this time? Does it really exist?"

She continued with her disdainful expression, shaking her head. "We gave you so many chances, Greg. Why couldn't you see the utopia that was being offered to you? I really, really wanted you as an Insider." She ushered him forward into the long, dark corridor. To his immediate left was a door marked 'Room 100'. She nodded towards it. He placed his hand on the handle and entered.

As his eyes adjusted to the low light level he became aware of another presence. Trish had entered behind him, but he could sense there was at least one other person in the room. A light came on, shining directly towards him. He raised his hand instinctively to shield his eyes.

"Gregor Workman, 4978-88-915689734." The voice sounded male, older, vaguely familiar. A stooped form stepped towards him and into the light. He was leaning on a cane. But even at full height he would not have exceeded 150 centimetres.

"Respected Vagrant Diversity 4989207!" said Greg in surprise.

"Div 498 is easier," replied the Respected Vagrant. "But then, again, I don't really mind either way. You can call even me 'My Lord', if it helps. Or why not Big Brother? I'm not bothered about names."

XVIII

"I don't think this is a time for humour, Div," replied Greg.

Div shrugged. "Big Brother, Div, even Zeus if you like. It makes no difference to me. They have given me many names, both formal and informal, over the years."

"Which side are you on?" asked Greg pointedly.

Div smiled. "In a war against entropy, who could ally themselves with chaos?"

"That's only if you accept the delusion that Conformity is an acceptable price to pay in order to slow social entropy," responded Greg.

"Delusion?" responded Div. "We think not. And while we're on the subject of price, dear boy, I'm rather afraid that you're about to discover how high the price of mismatching can rise." He raised his hand and another light came on behind him, a little to his left. "You might like to acquaint yourself with what's over there."

As Greg looked towards the place he was pointing, soft music began in the background. He could hear something familiar: an ancient instrument, a piano. With great expertise, someone was playing a piano. Then, as the volume rose to a level that was properly audible, he began to feel nausea rising from the pit of his stomach to his thorax. The soft, haunting tune was *Für Elise*.

"If you please," repeated Div, louder. The lighting level was gradually rising and Greg could see now that the room was much larger than he had realised. At the point where Div indicated was a table with 2 objects on it, each under a cover. Behind the table was a door in the sidewall of the room. The door was marked 'Room 101'.

"Are you starting to see, now, Greg?" asked Trish. "The

Department has been giving you chances to use your intelligence laterally for the last 15 years."

Greg's mind delved back through time, to his summons to Floor 7, Room 101. If that building had been laid out the same..."

"I know what you're thinking," continued Trish. "And yes, Floor 7 in the Permits Building was laid out in the same way as this one. All our buildings have a Floor 7 constructed identically."

The volume of music continued to rise.

"So, if I'd entered Room one hundred that day..." started Greg.

"You'd have found your way easily into Room 101," she finished for him. "It was an easy test, Greg. You were expected to pass it instantly. But because you failed..."

"The tests became more intrusive?" he interrupted.

"More... stimulating," she replied. "A randomly discovered book, or so it seemed to you. 2, in fact. A young girl draws the content of 1 to your attention. The other is written in a language which, had you taken the trouble to investigate, would have pointed you towards the events happening around you now. And if you had pursued further, there would have been other books in the same language – Kant's *Kritik*, Nietzsche's *Zarathustra*, Hitler's *Mein Kampf*. She shook her head disdainfully. "So much that could have been yours, Gregor, if only you had given yourself to it."

"Enough of this," interjected Div. "There is a purpose to your being here. Take the covers off the cages."

Greg noticed the use of the word 'cages' instantly. He lifted the 1st cover very slowly, very carefully. Under it there was indeed a cage. Inside the cage stood a birthday cake with a single burning candle on the top of it. He glanced back at Trish. Birthday cake and rats?" he enquired distastefully.

"Now, the other cover," instructed Div. Greg had barely disturbed it when something threw itself at the mesh of the cage from inside, shaking it violently. Only because it was anchored to the table did it not turn over.

Für Elise played on, now at a volume that was becoming intrusive.

Greg dropped the cover instantly. "No," he yelled almost involuntarily. "I will not subject myself to this humiliation."

"Oh, really?" enquired Div, his voice louder now, to carry above the music. "Then I can always do it for you. If I do, though, both of them will have their faces eaten by the rats. If you do it, one of them survives. And Greg, the great news is you get to choose which one!" The smile on Div's face was caustic, mocking.

"Both of who?" he asked. A deep flash of cold penetrated the pit of his stomach like a frozen blade.

Quite suddenly, the music stopped.

"Why, your wife or your son of course. You can save one of them but not both," replied Div.

Greg stood looking at him for a moment. There was not a hint of humour on the man's face. Then he looked at Trish, who was staring back at him intently. Greg shook his head at her in disbelief. "I'm truly sorry," she said. "I honestly didn't want it to come to this. I tried to tell you what forces you were playing with, but you wouldn't listen."

"Please," whispered Greg. "Please don't do this."

"But Greg, these are people you have already betrayed by your infidelity," replied Div. "You can't possibly be telling me it actually matters to you what happens to them. For all you knew until this precise moment, they had either drowned or they had been given prosthetic fish heads. How can you say you care which of them has their face eaten off and which survives?"

"Please, don't do this. Please don't harm my family. Please, where are they? Through here?" He ran, stumbling, to the door to Room 101 and reached towards the handle.

"Locked, I'm afraid, Greg. Locked until you make our decision.

Then, when 1 of the people you love has died, screaming in agony, the lock disengages automatically and you can enter the room. And there's more. If you want it, I promise you a boat and safe passage to leave with anyone still alive in there." Div stopped for a moment to let his words sink in. "Now, Co-Worker Greg Workman 4978-88-915689734. Take the cover off the rat cage, if you please, and let us begin."

Mutely, Greg moved forward towards the cages. With shaking hands, his arms outstretched and his face as far away as he could twist it, he carefully lifted the remaining cover. Three large grey rats screamed in execration, throwing themselves against the mesh. Greg drew back involuntarily, bent double and dropped the cover on the floor. He shuddered, close to vomiting.

"Thank you, Greg," said Div 498. "Now, concentrate please. Observe the channels." For the 1st time, Greg noticed a mesh corridor that led from the rats' cage to the wall that adjoined Room 101. At the wall, the channel forked into 2 before proceeding through into Room 101. Over one fork stood a plaque with the name 'Grete' above it. Over the other an identical plaque bore the name 'Joe'.

"Now, all you have to do, Greg," said Div 498, "is decide which of your loved ones receives the gift of the rats. And later, when that person has finished screaming and dying, you can take the cake to the survivor and, if you so wish, leave us forever. Now, is all that clear, Greg?"

He was weeping now, openly, uncontrollably. Whimpering and pleading, he dropped to his knees. "Please," he whispered between sobs. "I'll do anything for you. Please don't do this to my family."

"Oh, come now, my boy," replied Div 498, softening his tone in mock sympathy. "It really is best to get the decision over with. Then you can be off and start a new life with your wife. But then again... would she ever forget the terrified screams of her dying child as the rats ate his eyeballs? No, I suppose not. Better let her die then, and take your son. But... oh dear... to kill a young boy's mother right there in front of him in such a traumatic way. That can't be good for a child's psychological development either, can it? Why, he might even need to visit a Departmental therapist later in life. Dilemmas, Greg. Isn't life full of dilemmas? Now, make your choice." Div had been moving steadily closer to Greg as he spoke. And these last four words were screamed directly into his face.

Greg stood, still weeping uncontrollably. Slowly, he moved, shuffling towards the cages, closing in on the murder of one of the two people he cared about most in all the world. "Destroy," he mumbled. "They're making me destroy the only people I care about. This madness, utter madness." And at his own mumbled words, a tiny light came on inside his head. And the tiny light illuminated a half-forgotten phrase. Something she had said to him, in bed, was it? Something about destruction and madness. He reached inwardly for the light, for the words. A quote, but he had not recognised it, something by some long-forgotten poet about gods and destruction and madness. When he reached the cages, quite suddenly, he had it.

Whom the gods would destroy, they 1st make mad.

He thought through the words. The light grew from one candlepower to two. Then, with his hands hovering over the cages, he spoke the words softly to himself. "Whom the gods would destroy, they first make mad," he whispered. And the two candles became a hundred torches. And then he shouted the words, screamed them back in Div's face. "Whom the gods would destroy, they first make mad." And the hundred torches burned with the light of ten million lumens. "I know you, you, wily old bastard!

And I know your game. Respected Vagrant, Diversity 4989207, Div 498, My Lord, Big Brother, Zeus, if your insatiable narcissism demands it. I don't give a shit, you Fucker. Your game is utterly and completely up! I don't love you and I never will. I don't love you, Big Brother. I don't love you!"

And with that, he reached forward and raised the mesh divides that separated the rats from the birthday cake. In less than a second, they stormed in upon it in a frenzy of flying cake and fur and blood as they scrambled over one another to get to the maddening sweetness of the food in their ravenous hunger. The tears still streaming down his face, Greg strode to the door to Room 101 and reached for the handle. It was unlocked, as he knew beyond doubt it would be. He threw it open, banging it hard enough against the partition wall to make it shake violently.

Burning with rage, he turned back to Div 498. Pointing into the room and with tears, glorious triumphant tears streaming down his face, tears of anger and of relief and of agony and of joy, "It's empty, Div. It's fucking empty," he screamed. "Can you see that, Div? It's empty. And do you know why it's empty, Div? Sure you do. It's because there is no human being inside it. And for that reason, and that reason alone, it contains everything I ever wanted to see. Fuck your Compliance and your sanitised, insipid books and your rewritten history and your evil-hearted pestiferous, pontificating superiority. It's fucking empty, Div and there's nothing you can ever, ever, do to make me love you."

Later, he stood in the boat as it rocked gently against the jetty where she was standing. He watched the water as it lapped against the wall of the half-submerged building. "I told him you'd work it out," said Trish. "I told him he couldn't break you."

"And my family?" he asked.

"I'm sorry, Greg, but we don't know. We never did. Perhaps they drowned, perhaps they escaped – we know some did. I can't help you any further with that. I'm sorry."

"You know I'll never stop looking for them, don't you?" he answered as he untied the boat and turned the ignition.

"Poor Greg," she replied, genuinely sympathetic this time. "Still looking for a home for other gods."

Greg shook his head. "Not other gods," he replied, as he turned the boat around.

"Titans."

Other Books by Michael Forester

If It Wasn't For That Dog

It's Amazing What You Can Achieve with Persistence, A Bit of Chopped Liver and a Second-Hand Teddy Bear...

In 2002 Michael, a deafened man from the New Forest, lost his home, his marriage, his business and his father – but then again, he always was a tad careless. However, in the same year, someone suggested that getting a dog might be a good idea – not just any dog, but a hearing dog from Hearing Dogs for Deaf People. And when, in 2004, Michael was presented with a Hearing Dog of his own called Matt, he just knew life would be so much easier. Amazing how wrong you can be, isn't it!

If It Wasn't For That Dog is the story of Matt's first year with Michael, the challenges and accomplishments of climbing the Hearing Dog learning curve, the profound changes he stimulated and the inestimable joy he confers magically on everyone who meets him. But most of all, it is the story of the strange power of meaty treats to work miracles in doggie behaviour.

Dragonsong

Sometimes Nothing but the Death of Your Father Will Do

Rebekah, noblewoman of Albion, has been driven to madness by the murder of her lover Vidar. In her torment she bargains with the Prince of Demons to turn her into a dragon. Thus transformed, she seeks to take revenge upon her father, Merlin, whom she is fooled into believing is responsible for Vidar's death. To save the world from the ravages of Dragonsong, Merlin is forced to banish his beloved daughter to Hell, regardless of the consequences for him personally. Behind the subterfuge stands Oberon, Captain-King of Elves. He does not foresee the devastation his jealousy and unrequited love for Rebekah will unleash upon Gaia when he frees her from Merlin's spell and summons her from Hell to support his war against Albion. To save Gaia a second time, Merlin is forced to travel back in time to prepare a warrior capable of overcoming the dragon through the power of the Sleep Stone. But he does not foresee the bond that will develop between the dragon and his own assistant, the Seer, Michael of Albion. If Lady Attie and Michael prove unable to return the Sleep Stone to the mouth of Hell in time, the Demon Army will be swarm out of Hell and overrun Gaia. Time. Time is the key. Time is the only solution to Gaia's destiny – but only if the gods of Asgard can find a way to stop it.

The Goblin Child

Well, hello there.

Why don't you step inside and take a look round? You remember this place, don't you? That's right. You've been here before. And us. Surely you remember us. We're old friends. This is where the light in your eyes glimpses the darkness in your mind.

Sit down and stay a while – if you can face the risk of finding out who you really are, that is. I'll introduce you to some friends of mine:

Meet the man who remembers his birth. He wishes he didn't.
- And the goblin child – if his mother is to be believed.
- Or how about the boy who takes his god to school?
- Here's Madeleine, the author who can't get beyond chapter seven – because of the raven with white eyes, that is.
- And Santa. Yes, you really must meet Santa.
- But really it's all about David, who spent his life circling the moon – just like you and I do, in fact
- Come with me. Come with me now.

Forest Rain
Spiritual Learnings for a New Age

Your spiritual journey is unique to you. But it is in mindfulness of the journeys of those who travel with us that we learn more of our own purpose and how we can draw energy and meaning from the challenges and events on our road.

This collection of Spiritual Learnings in prose and poetry form a unique meditation that will support you in exploring your own journey, and the life events, both great and small, that will offer themselves to you as you travel forward.

These meditations will move you to joy; they will move you to tears. They will help you give yourself permission to experience the depth of learning to be found within, to experience fully what you have come into the world to learn and to teach. In so doing, they will support you in discovering the astonishing and profound messages meant for you alone, for *Forest Rain* truly is your Heart's Home.

Biographical

Michael Forester is a deafened writer who lives in Hampshire's
New Forest with his hearing dog, Matt.

He can be contacted at michaelforesterauthor@gmail.com

Michael Forester with hearing dog Matt.